Time Was

D0048569

BOOKS BY IAN MCDONALD

LUNA TRILOGY
Luna: New Moon
Luna: Wolf Moon
Luna: Moon Rising (forthcoming)

EVERNESS SERIES
Planesrunner
Be My Enemy
Empress of the Sun

INDIA IN 2047
River of Gods
Cyberabad Days

CHAGA SAGA
Chaga
Kirinya
Tendeléo's Story

DESOLATION ROAD SERIES
Desolation Road

Ares Express

TIME
WAS

✦ ✦ ✦

IAN
McDONALD

A TOM DOHERTY ASSOCIATES BOOK

NEW YORK

This is a work of fiction. All of the characters, organizations, and events portrayed in this novella are either products of the author's imagination or are used fictitiously.

TIME WAS

Copyright © 2018 by Ian McDonald

Cover photograph of two men on a rural road © Stephen Mulcahey/Arcangel, cover photograph of night sky © Getty Images
Cover design by Christine Foltzer

Edited by Jonathan Strahan

A Tor.com Book
Published by Tom Doherty Associates
175 Fifth Avenue
New York, NY 10010

www.tor.com

Tor® is a registered trademark of
Macmillan Publishing Group, LLC.

ISBN 978-0-7653-9145-2 (ebook)
ISBN 978-0-7653-9146-9 (trade paperback)

First Edition: April 2018

Time Was

We kiss and the sea catches fire.

Spitalfields

They came like vultures, hesitant, hovering, drawn by the pheromone of dying books. Many I knew—the dealer world is a small one. Tall Lionel in that same charcoal suit, shiny at ass and elbow, working the plastic bins like a hunting heron: perfect stillness, the stab down snatch up of a cloth-bound volume. Louisa in Louboutins, wearing a dust mask, her heels and trademark red soles teeter-tottering around in the dumpster as she flicked over broken-backed volumes with a litter-picker. She feared fungi that grew in the bindings of old, damp books. Terry Prentice-Hall. I thought he died years ago. I'm sure I went to his funeral. Still questing for the mythical Harry Potter first editions. Some faces I knew by repute: Nancy and Flea, the Parasites of Enfield. Q. R. Rice, wafted in from Oxford. His cotton manuscript gloves left no one in any doubt that Spitalfields was unendurable to anyone of refinement. Some I did not know by face or gossip: a woman and man in their twenties throwing academic textbooks into a wheelbarrow. "Charity workers," Tall Lionel wheezed. For a big man, he moved quietly. I hadn't seen him slide in close to my ear. "They send them to Africa, India, some needy shit-hole. Fuck me sideways, there's Niall Rudd. Last I heard he was doing three years in Ford. Always was a shite forger."

Some were not even dealers. I recognized Martin Parr, the photographer; that Spitalfields blogger and his cat; Dan Cruickshank, the architectural historian and television presenter. The Golden Page first opened its doors in 1933: it had long been a beating organ of Spitalfields.

I have drunk the legendary Vietnamese coffee and supped the sulphurous vegetable broth on the collapsing sofas. I have sat through poetry readings when I couldn't afford the electricity at home, I have sat through fifty shades of red political theorists and jeered Bliar Blair and his warmongering. I have huddled over the gas heater on February evenings, high on carbon monoxide. I have dragged myself up through Saturday hangovers to comb through the house clearances as they arrived out of the back of a van: first refusal on anything with a hint of war about it. That was my specialism, the Second World War. You specialize. There are too many books in the world. Tall Lionel hunted old SF paperbacks, Chris Foss covers preferred. Louisa in Louboutins dealt in crime, the pulpier the better. War for me, in hardback. There will always be a market for war.

Now The Golden Page was dead. The stock Richie

could not flog even at ten for a pound was stacked in plastic boxes, on trestle tables, dumped in a steel skip on Folgate Street under a quick November sky threatening rain. The Liberty has always been a liminal place, caught between the City and the city, a gutter of refuge, a huddle of difference, pressed from both sides. Jews and Huguenots. The towers of finance and Banglatown. Gentrification won. Richie had been unable to resist the offer for the building. I would have too. Fuck Vietnamese coffee. Cappuccino in Umbria for Richard Frowse.

When we were sated, when we could stomach no more books, Tall Lionel suggested the Hawksmoor, to raise a glass to the old place, but I was dispirited by my colleagues, by their small-minded acquisitiveness, by the weather, by the thin drizzle now turning old book covers to pulp in the slowly filling dumpster. I wanted away from these ghastly fossils. I was of a different generation from my colleagues, but I understood that irst day when I caught another acquisitive eye working the stacks in Clapham High Street War on Want: this would be my cohort, my college, my congregation, for the rest of my professional life. Fingers around hot whisky on a cold evening, carping and moaning about postage charges, eBay T&Cs and PayPal's ever-increasing transaction times.

I made my excuses. Loot to log, titles to research, purchases to post. And the possibility of wonder. My chilled fingers had detected a discontinuity in the bound leaves of one of my acquisitions, an otherwise unremarkable and, to me, unknown book of poetry; *Time Was*. By E.L. Anonymous initials were enough to trigger my curiosity, as was the date. May 1937, Ipswich. No publisher listed. Decent paper, hand-stitched binding, header tapes in fair order and good fabric binding. Gold-leaf low-relief of an hourglass, half run through. As a free book, a dumpster find, it was worth picking up. But my fingers had sensed something more rare and valuable: an inclusion. A bookmark, perhaps from a long-dead English-language bookshop in a European capital—perhaps farther afield. Istanbul. Cairo. Perhaps a hand-stitched sampler, marking a page. A postcard. A love letter. Dried flowers; a nosegay, a posy, a rose clipped the night before battle. Photographs; best of all with love, with signatures, with farewells. Provenances, I called them. If they were connected with the book—a history of a campaign, a military biography, a popular, long-out-of-print thriller or crime story mentioned in the letter or card--I sold them. They added value. The orphans, the refugees, I kept.

The Tube was crowded and smelly. I let the book fall open where the insertion demanded. The smell of fusty paper, damp cover binding, obliterated the stink of fast food and electricity.

A letter. A single sheet, still creased from the envelope despite years between pages. My hands shook as I read it.

Dear Ben,

I watched the lights along the Western Harbour drop away until they merged with the dark horizon. I made the taxi driver take me out along Al Max until I could see the lights no more. I never thought they would take you away like this, in a troopship. I suppose His Majesty needs his photo-boy more than I do. I suppose we should have made more of the time. We never do. We become so lazy in love. But love is laziness, the gift of each other's time, to spendthrift or invest. I remember your arms, I remember dreadful gin, I remember the perfume of your hair. Your skin smells of honey. Those precious times—those precious rooms—at Osborne House and the Heliopolis Club. Rev Anson always suspected.

The barrage balloons are going up all along the Corniche. The air is wonderfully still, I swear I can hear the guns from the front. Light sparks along the western horizon. Christ knows what's happening out there. It reminds me of Russia, when all we could do was watch the world burn.

In three nights I fly. I know what you'd say: Alex

is the oldest of pleasure-cities: be bright, be gay, drink more of the dreadful gin, drink a skinful. This city holds no attractions for me. Next to you, its pleasures are dry and stale. I need to be where you are, wherever you are. Ironic that I will leave later yet arrive before you.

I fear the next translation is not far off—you develop a sense for it, like smelling a storm. I dread being apart from you. Should we become separated, I'll leave a copy behind me, here in the usual place.

Time was, time will be again,
Tom

Shingle Street

I have lived twenty years on this street of stones. I have known it in all seasons and all elements, in its many temperaments.

I know it in the easterlies, when the sky is black as judgment and the wind seems to strip the land back like skin peeling from a jaw and the sea drives hard onto the shingle and the knock of rolling pebbles becomes a thunder so great I can hear it from Ferry Road.

I know it in snow, those rare days of undifferentiated grey when the turnstones face into the white whip of thin flakes thrown down from the Baltic, when each pebble wears a rind of snow, locked together by ice. How many pebbles from Bawdsey to Orford Ness? There are people who could number that, but I am not one of them.

I know it in rain, when it becomes an undulating black river, shiny as a swimming dog, and the boats, the nets, the huts and row houses and the Martello tower seem to hunker down from it, seeking shelter in a shelterless terrain.

I know it in high summer sun, when the sky and sea

seem anchored together and the whole world lies exhausted between them and nothing stirs, even breathes, when sky is heavy as tidewater and the sea seems to lift free from mere geography. On those days Shingle Street is a broad blade of forged iron, and in the evening, the gulls lift on a wind only they can perceive.

In every mood, I take the bike out and ride the road of sea-rounded stones.

There's a skill to it, and an art. The skill is riding a 1938 Ariel Red Hunter at speed on a road of treacherous cobbles that could shift and spill you at any time. The art is reading the stones: what is constant, what has changed, what has moved where in conjunction with what. This is a landscape rolled and moved by the tides, each pebble lifted and dropped, lifted and dropped by the run and ebb, each advance and retreat carried a little farther upcoast. It is never the same twice.

~

I usually ride out to where the pebbles end and the Orford's sweet waters and the salt North Sea run into each other in eddies and silver swirls. But today I feel the presence of war like a weather front. The sky is clogged with contrails, the straight lines of the bombers, the circles and spirals of the fighters looping around them. Felixstowe took it three nights in a row. The Luftwaffe has moved on to Ipswich. Sky and sea feel polluted, stained and impure. I leave the bike by the Martello tower and walk up the beach towards the abandoned village. I peer through the window of one of the empty row houses. The tenants were evicted hastily. Overlooked things remain: cutlery in the kitchen, a loaf in the bread bin now a cube of blue mold, newspapers and coal under the stairs, calendars on the wall, permanently stalled at May 15, 1940. I shiver, a sudden feeling that I have somehow affronted the house, that the people who lived there, wherever they are, felt my intrusion and glared.

Vapor trails in the sky, the nightly flicker of anti-aircraft fire, rumors of barges massing along the coast of Holland, Kriegsmarine minesweepers probing the Channel defenses. This is the invasion coast.

I like it better empty. Emptied. When I came here as a boy, when I wandered and met and learned from E.L., I saw their faces pressed to these same windows, frowning out. Who was on their land, in their view, on their horizon. Suspicious, possessive people. Sandings folk. A landscape of grey resentments and long grudges. Gone now. Moved out. Fuck them. This is mine now.

E.L. would have liked it.

I have his book with me. I'm seldom apart from it; it

sits neatly in the pocket of my service dress, as if tailored to it. Flap buttoned down, pressed against the heart. I take no comfort from its close presence today. There is war in every element, and I'm unsettled, itchy, headachy, like I used to be before a storm.

No images here. Nothing to take back and try to wrestle down onto a page. Sea and stone have said enough to me. I kick the engine to life and ride back through the deepening twilight. My blackout headlight is a slot of wan light.

~

War is no reason to change your drinking habits. I've been frequenting the Swan at Alderton since I was a fourteen-year-old selling fire lighters door to door up and down the Sandings. "Frequenting": an old man's word, thumbs in the waistcoat, arse to the fire. I know the beer; I know the landlord; I know the seasons and the temperaments. I used to be able to sit quietly in the window seat, or on the bench under the same window in the long summer, and whittle away at words, frown over rhyme schemes and assonances. Sometimes I read; sometimes I just sit, in the sun, like an old man. The girls from the Receiver Block come here, to the consternation of landlord Rydal, who considers women in his pub a trump of doomsday, also those of the enlisted men and the re-search divisions who find the messes too raucous and loutish.

"Ahoy, Tom the Rhymer," they greet me. I can hear the capitalizations. I smile, nod. I know I'm a figure of fun and that some detest me for imagined pretensions. I'm thought odd, even for Signals. I accept the ribbing, the murmurs. It's a wooden decoy duck, staked to the bot-tom of the fen. It's pleading guilty to a minor charge to escape a greater one.

The radar girls swing up the lane, dressed and made up, Victory rolls and painted-on stocking seams, chatter-ing and laughing. From my summer bench with a sun-warmed pint on the end I admire their loud confidence. War has been the making of them, saved them from mar-riage or service or other menial drudgeries. They greet me from afar.

"What are you working on?" Lizzie always hails me.

I lift the notebook.

"War, time and memory," I say. She grins. Attempted art does not embarrass her. She knows me. I know it. You know these things. She isn't distracted by the decoy.

"Pint for the Rhymer," Lizzie commands Rydal. Arms linked, the radar girls march three abreast into the back room from which they have expelled the old drinking men and which they have claimed with the flag of RAF

Bawdsey RDF Receivers, until kingdom come or war end, amen.

There's always a pint for the poet.

I can hear Charlie Nair from five fields away. I should imagine those stealthy Kriegsmarine minesweepers can hear him, out on the shallow sea. "You need to sort your chain," I tell him. "It'll break and take your leg off clean below the knee. Let me do it." I could do it easily, ten minutes' work. Charlie won't let me. I don't know Nortons, he says. I know Nortons and I know Charlie and he never will allow me to fix it. It would be a humiliation.

He pulls up in a clatter and racket and smoke and pushes up his goggles. I have to admit he rides that abused Norton well.

"Anyone got a round in?" he always asks. I never have. I never will. It's my Norton drive chain. He leaves the bike lying in the hedge and bangs down beside me on my bench. I barely snatch my pint to safety. Now I can hear the engines of the main drinking party and glimpse the green roofs of their cars over the hedge lines. There are two more cars than usual.

"We're breaking in the new boys," Charlie announces. The drinking party arrives in white dust.

I remember. I carried the dispatches myself. A new research division was moving into the Dairy. There had been rumors of secret projects, new ways of sensing, seeing the distant and concealed.

Car doors opened. New boots on the gravel. The scientists looked uncomfortable in uniform. All but one. Oh, one. One whose boots were firmly planted. One who wore the uniform like skin, like the sky, who stood tall and certain and lifted his hands to his eyes when he stared at this place he had been taken, who shaded his eyes and so could not see me staring. Staring as if there were nothing else in the world, staring like a radar girl at a lone blip on my screen, my stare reaching out across the world and returning an echo. Until he dropped his hand and I was not quick enough to look away—deliberately so—and his eye caught mine. We knew. We communicated through the airwaves. Then he was swept through the door into beery camaraderie: Boffins Corner, we called it, and I sat on my bench with my beer in the long evening sun and all my notes, all my words and rhymes and rhythms and images, all my thoughts and all the things I held in my heart, were nothing.

Clapham

I missed my stop. I missed the stop after.

There were enough clues in the letter for me to place and roughly date it. The references to Osborne House and the Heliopolis Club immediately identified Cairo; Al Max and the Western Harbour landmarked Alexandria. The line about hearing the guns placed the time around either the first or second battle of El Alamein. The front was only eighty kilometers west of Alexandria—Montgomery's line in the sand—and on a still night, across the waters of Mareotis, notorious for how they warped sounds and closed up spaces so that a distant conversation was as intimate as a whisper, it would be possible to hear the artillery. I can't imagine any troops being rotated home in British Egypt's darkest hour, so I inclined more towards the Second Battle of El Alamein in October. A place and a time. Five minutes online would give me the British order of battle in Egypt in 1942. I glanced again at the letter. *I suppose His Majesty needs his photo-boy more than I do.* Ben served in Intelligence. This would be fun. It was then that I realized I had dreamed through my stops, and I regained enough presence of mind to push onto the platform as the doors were closing.

A love letter. Every war is a profound sexual revolution. Social mores are upset, norms overturned. Tucked into the end paper of Bill Slim's *Defeat into Victory* I found a photograph of a couple in khakis before the Taj Mahal: the brief scrawl on the back hinted at love across class, religion, country. Slipped between the pages of a September 1942 final edition of *Film Fun* I discovered a gloriously uninhibited sexual fantasy of a Lincolnshire Land Girl for her Brooklyn Bomber Boy. Now, within a volume of small-press verse: Tom and Ben. Solid, unromantic monosyllables, dull as a spade. Twenty lines, yet they conjured up such a world to me: another love fertilized by the thrilling otherness of wartime Alexandria. The streets and souks opened into universes of possibility.

Costa was still open. I found my customary table closest to the Wi-Fi router. I photographed the book and the letter and prepared them for my vendor site, AbeBooks and eBay. A house party rocked the street with slow dub. In the bass and drum I saw barrage balloons sagging over the Corniche, two men clinking martini glasses at the bar of the Cap D'Or, grimacing at the dreadful gin. I saw them kiss in the dark of an alley, beneath an awning. I imagined Hurricanes roaring overhead. I took the letter down and clicked *post*. I wondered what became of Tom and Ben. Too many of the war loves I had followed did not survive. Peace killed them. People returned to their old lives and loves; quickly the old order reasserted itself, the very order for which they had fought.

A cursory search turned up nothing, but I hadn't expected much. Photoreconnaissance was a classified area, and however romantic I found the idea of Ben flying out over the desert in the nose of a Blenheim light bomber, he was much more likely to have served in Interpretation. Or something more intriguing; Intelligence covered more esoteric and romantic disciplines, all spiced with the clandestine and therefore quite irresistible to me.

The poetry book sold before I was even through my first coffee. It made a decent price. I lingered until Michaela stockaded me in upturned chairs, and dragged back to the flat. Police were arriving as I was departing. Two squad cars and a van with grids over the windows, to shut down a noisy dub party.

Flat, I say. Two rooms with shared kitchen and bathroom back of Littlebury Street. One room filled floor to ceiling with books, the other filling, pushing me deeper into the corner by the window. I slept among the tombstones of ancient wars. Mea culpa, mea maxima culpa: I broke the rule to never use what you push. I loathed my rooms; I gave them as little time as I could. Rona my landlady wanted me out—she could get six hardworking

Somali boys in my two rooms—but was too lazy to pursue it with anything approaching zeal. She claimed she was worried about the health and safety implications of my stacks collapsing and burying me. I knew she feared the weight of books was slowly warping her ceiling joists. She pushed the rent up religiously; I scraped and traded and paid. I dreaded having to carry several thousand books, double-rowed, down four flights of stairs. She dreaded having to help me.

I have become fixed in my customary vices. I work and read into the early morning; I sleep long and rise late. Book dealing is a business best conducted from your own bed. In the deep three o'clock, four o'clock, there is something old and feral and rather beautiful about Clapham. The wind seems to blow from a direction not marked on any compass; new, fresh, music carries far on it, imbued with a lonely splendor I never hear in the flat, tinny light.

I worked into the morning, diving deeper into regimental histories and the more obsessive corners of amateur military history. Mysteries you were, Tom and Ben. Leads turned blind; avenues of inquiry ran into blank walls, like a city lost in the dunes. Finally, as the dawn crept up the sky and the clatter and boom of commuter trains ousted the night musics, I posted the whole thing to Facebook—a dozen bibliophile and war history groups—and rolled into my bed.

I woke with my face in full, painful sunshine, Rona telling me the man had come about the wiring, and the ping of an answer in my notifications. Out on East Anglia Desert Rats Facebook Page, someone had recognized Tom and Ben.

~

Thorn Hildreth. A name to savor, a name that invited speculation, especially out in West Pinchbeck. *Incest and line dancing,* Tall Lionel had declared of the flatlands of Lincolnshire, before adding, *motor sport.* And, latterly, *Brexit.*

Whoever Thorn might be, her great-grandfather had bequeathed her an attic of wartime memories: the Reverend Anson Hildreth's diaries of his chaplaincy in 1940s Egypt. Her comment had shone through a bottomless scroll of *toucheds* and *weeping nows* and *so beautifuls* and heart emoticons attached to my post of Tom's letter to Ben. She knew these names. She recalled a passage, a photograph. Might I like to come to see the relevant parts of the archive?

Might I like to? Not, *did I want to?*

I'm a man much charmed by quaint turns of speech.

Fenland

Thorn picked me up from Spalding Station in a decaying Volvo station wagon that smelled of damp, dog and stale patchouli. Moss grew along the window seals. I could watch moving road through a hole in the footwell. I knew from her profile that she was of an age with me, though her piercings and tattoos were alarmingly alien. She was shorter than my imagining, stocky in her skinny jeans, a T-shirt that carried the legend *Fenlands Lioness* and a biker jacket. Patchouli failed to mask the feral perfume of someone who spent much time with animals.

"Thorn. The thirtieth letter of the Icelandic alphabet," I said. She did not take my conversational bait.

"That's Moulton Mill," she said, nodding across the flat, unhedged fields to the white-capped brick tower. The sails had been furled for winter.

"The tallest windmill in Britain," I said.

"Working mill," Thorn said. "The tallest mill is probably—"

"Bixley," I said. "Truncated from eleven floors to seven."

She looked at me. I had passed her test of geekdom.

Thorn pointed out every windmill, stump and post and tower along the Doverhirne Drain into West Pinchbeck. I had hoped she would let me study the documents in situ; then when I smelled the car I hoped not to see the inside of her house; was alarmed as we headed past scattered fen-side hamlets into puritan flatness, then relieved when we turned into the car park of the New Bridge Inn beside a pumping station. She heaved two plastic boxes out of the back of the car and led me into the snug. The carpets smelled of overused vacuum cleaner bags. The Polish woman at the bar knew Thorn and brought decent IPAs. Thorn spread her material on the table.

Photographs, letters, diaries and notebooks.

"Greygram was a padre with the Royal Army Chaplains' Department," she said.

"Greygram?"

"Great-grandfather."

"Is that a Fens word?"

"No, it's our word."

The Fens raise strange children. The Hildreths traced back to fourteenth-century Berkshire but set roots in the silt lands in the elbow of the Wash in the midseventeenth century. They crowned their lives with stern, elemental Anglo-Saxon names. Reverend Anson's son Leland, Thorn's grandfather, eschewed his father's quiet Anglicanism and joined Raymond Buckland in Nottingham in the early sixties to explore Anglo-Saxon paganism. When Buckland settled permanently in the USA, Leland Hildreth took the tenets of Seax-Wica and further antiqued them by burying them deep and dark in Fenland culture. His Hilderwic paganism attracted a few notoriety seekers and the attention of the local press, but there weren't enough true devotees for it to cohere and the papers lost interest when they discovered there was no nudity. Hilderwic collapsed in mutual adulteries and backbitings. Pagans are worse than Protestants for denominationalism. Toland, Thorn's father, moved to Peterborough, where he worked in motorbike repair. Thorn detested Toland's girlfriend—she had split Thorn from her mother—and had moved back into the Hildreth manse in West Pinchbeck, where she cared for the ailing Leland, four dogs, three cats, a pony, a donkey, an attic full of the military archives of Rev Anson and the founder and collected theology of Hilderwic paganism.

"Greygram always felt guilty that he never fought in the First World War," Thorn said over the second pint. "The day after war was declared, he signed up. My gram never forgave him. Greygram abandoned him; Granna Hild and Grunc Adric left my greygranna Maudie to run the parish. She did the rounds on a bike, visiting his parishioners. They survived on food parcels from the De

Eresby estate, while he swanned around Cairo and Alexandria with a peaked cap and a swagger stick. He broke an ankle in a car crash in 1943 and it never reset properly. Came back on a stick and insisted everyone treat him like a war hero. He never once thanked my greygranna for everything she did. Some people had a fucking cushy war. I sometimes think Leland started the whole Hilderwic thing just to piss Greygram off."

"He kept the archive."

"Would have been too much effort to throw it out. Not a great man for effort, Gram. Someone has to hold on to it all."

And here were two more pints. Small, fierce Thorn opened up the diaries—beautiful, fragrant things bound in a leather as soft as an infant's instep.

"This is from March 1941. Greygram had just been transferred to Cairo and attached to the Ninth Heavy Anti-Aircraft Regiment."

"The Londonderries."

She took a sip of the ale. It left an adorable moustache on her upper lip. I yearned to wipe it away.

"This is his introduction to the Heliopolis Club."

As a diarist, the Reverend Anson was a fine sermonizer. The bibliophile learns to check her contemporary sensibilities when reading old books—particularly personal or private accounts—but I found the Reverend Anson's Anglican indignation at the Cairenes patronizing and tiring. He must have been a dreary preacher. The entry concluded with his naked gloating at being unanimously voted into wartime Cairo's elite sporting club. *Tennis tomorrow! I must have my batman press my whites. Hoorah, Rev Hildreth!*

"For a man of the cloth he's a fearsome snob," I ventured.

"He's a shit in a surplice," Thorn said with venom. "And worse, as you'll find out. I think this is what you're looking for."

She passed me another soft tan notebook. The hand was small and slanted, written at speed in the way of a man who wrote much, but clear and legible.

May 25th, 1941

Something simply must be done about the greens. The boys hand-water them every night, but all that results from that is arcs of verdure that describe the range of their watering cans while the remainder is tufts of desiccated grass or bare dust. Getting a decent lie is impossible. To hazard a putt on those abominations is more like seaside fun-golf than the noble and ancient game.

Stayed over at the club again last night. After the big storm two nights ago the Italians have resumed raids—not bound for us this time, though the Eyties are not beyond dumping their load prematurely if they think the target is too hot, and skedaddling for home. The Canal Zone again, dropping mines. We did what we usually did, blacked out and retired to the bar and, when the electricity went down, which it inevitably does during the raids, drank by candlelight. An agreeable evening, until the AA batteries on Zamalek opened up and Cowan felt compelled to ask me, "Are those your boys?" He knew as well as I that the Paddies were stationed at Sidi Bishr. He never misses an opportunity to jibe when I am not with my unit, though I have made pains to explain that, as Ministers of Christ, we enjoy a peripatetic brief. I do not care for Cowan. He is quick to criticise, loath to praise; he finds a worm in every rose: the very model of a cynic. I took my drink out onto the cricket pitch where Carmichael and Peters joined me and we sat in the balmy night air, watching the explosions of the ack-ack rounds and the play of the searchlight beams against the sky. Cairo is a smoky, dusty hole, but in the blackout it catches something of the starry magnificence of the skies at Abu Simbel. I had hoped that storm would have dropped a goodly plump of rain on our poor, suffering greens, but it was some uncanny Egyptian thing, roiling clouds and hot winds, strange illuminations and dry lightning. Nary a spit of rain.

Towards midnight Tom roared in on an Enfield—Lord knows where he had commandeered it, let alone how he had navigated Cairo in a blackout. He had a pillion passenger, a sallow, dark-haired lad, rather sloppy in his dress, I thought. His insignia—a sphinx and the motto *Vigilant*—was not familiar to me. Photoreconnaissance, Cowan later informed me. RAF. That explained the general slovenliness. Tom pulled off his riding gloves, banged the dust out of them and bellowed for a gin and tonic. The pillion passenger introduced himself as Ben Seligman. He carried no baggage but a single book: some rum, arty thing about time.

"Ben's down from Malta," Tom declared, slinging an arm around the chap. "Flew in this night. My oldest, dearest friend. I haven't seen him in . . . Christ knows. Sorry, Padre."

I have never seen a fellow so gay as Tom with his old friend. He ordered champagne for everyone—Royal Engineers are well paid, certainly better than chaplains, but not so wealthy as to splash champagne with pharaonic excess. As he and Ben were soon to head down the Delta, he proposed an excursion to the pyramids, which we, rendered amiable by much champagne, did not refuse, though I detest the venal aggression of the hawkers. They retired early—Tom had booked rooms. The guns opened up again; the Eyeties were returning from the Canal Zone.

"A reader," Carmichael said with distaste, knocking

the dottle from his pipe against the leg of the deck chair, where it fell in glowing red twists. He was an avid sportsman; even I hovered on the edge of the dangerously intellectual to him. "Poetry."

"A Son of Shem," Peters said.

I said, "I do hope Tom isn't thinking of proposing him for the club."

"Tom said they were going down to Alex."

"Good," I said. "I should so hate to have to blackball him."

The searchlights sprang to life again and for a brief instant we saw the silhouette of a Sparviero caught between the beams. Then the guns spoke again and the night filled with explosions. By the time we had all agreed that a nightcap really should be the thing, the all clear was sounding.

"I sold a copy of a poetry book titled *Time Was*," I said. In my time in the heat and dust of wartime Cairo, Lincolnshire had grown cold and dark. Condensation beaded the snug window, breaking the light from the car park into lager-colored pearls. "The letter was inside it. Ben must have given it to Tom in Alexandria."

"Look."

Thorn slid a photograph across the table. A group of six soldiers posed in front of the Sphinx, lolling in Sidi

Barrani shorts, open-necked shirts, socks around their ankles. Gleeful with the fragile happy-go-lucky energy of young people in wartime: all but one tall man at the end of the line, a pace distant from the others, as if to mark a vital social distinction, sober of face, dressed in pressed long pants, a clerical collar visible at the neckline of his shirt.

At the other end of the line, a grinning man in dark glasses leaned on the shoulder of his neighbor. His skin was pale, untouched by Ra.

"That must be Ben," I said. "Seligman?" And the man on whom he leaned: "Tom?"

"The names are on the back," Thorn said.

Ben Seligman, Tom Chappell, Norman Carmichael, Brian Cowan, James Caterham, Rev Hildreth. Penciled in a neat, Anglican hand.

Thorn laid out two more photographs; the same actors: with camels, with the Great Pyramid, astride tiny donkeys. I ran my fingers along the scalloped edges of the prints, a tactile pleasure of old photographs I have always loved.

"That's them," Thorn said. "I'm sure of it. But . . ."

I have never been able to resist the word "but." It's the ragged edge of the photograph, the texture of a provenance disturbing the flat perfection of a book.

"There is a . . . ," Thorn began.

"Mystery?" I finished.

"I checked the service records of everyone in photore-connaissance in the western desert. There is no record of anyone by the name of Ben Seligman, either PRU or ISLD."

I shivered. It could have been the big fen country night had taken a step closer to me. Most of it was delight. This was what every dealer, every bibliophile, craved: a story outside the book.

"Do you think he was a spy or something?"

Thorn nodded.

Then I said very carefully, "Do you mind if I show these to someone?"

She drew back, frowned, and my heart turned over. I feared I had taken a liberty too far. I had appropriated her family history.

"Who?"

"Someone I know in the Imperial War Museum in London. She's in the photographic archive."

"She?"

"Shahrzad."

Thorn looked dubious.

"She has a gift."

"A what?"

"A talent."

Thorn's eyes widened. For a moment I worried I had

asked too much, pushed too far.

"I won't let you take any of the archive."

"Can I photograph a few things?"

She nodded.

"Don't share them."

"Only Shahrzad."

As I closed the camera app I noticed the time. I had twenty minutes until I was stranded in rural Fenlandia. Thorn drove me to the station. She should not have been driving. She should not have been anywhere near a car. She blasted along the straight fen-country roads, headlights blazing, horn blaring when she took the narrow bridges. I made the train as the gate was closing. I was still drunk as the train pulled into King's Cross, haunted by a momentary glimpse into a mystery seventy-five years old and the lingering perfume of patchouli.

Shingle Street

Under a sky the color of judgment I pushed the bike hard up Shingle Street, throttles open, threatening the stones to spill me, to strip the meat from my bones as I rolled and skidded over the pebbles.

You man you man, go away, get out of my heart leave me alone.

When I came up here when I was a boy and we met before the tower, E.L. sometimes put his hands over my eyes.

"What are you experiencing?"

"Nothing."

"Really? What are you feeling?"

A giggle.

"Silly. Your hands."

More.

The smell of salt, stones recently wet by rain. The movement of air over my skin, how it changed moment by moment, the stir of the hairs on my bare legs. The cry of gulls, voice beyond voice all the way to the horizon. The rolling knock of pebbles. The sound of my breathing. The particular smell of soap from your hand.

If you want to write, you must write experience. What it is to be that thing. There is everything in a moment.

My experience? Love, as suddenly it leaves me gasping for breath, so sharp it is a spear run through my belly.

I leave the Ariel on its side in the marram grass and trudge down to the tide line to pick up stones and fling them as hard and far out to sea as I can. I could do it for a thousand years and Shingle Street would not be a stone lessened. The sea would roll them in again, tide by tide, storm by storm.

I kick the bike back to life and race up the beach, roaring at the emptied houses.

~

Now I understand. This is what poetry is for. This is why it exists. No gods, no muses, no *inspiration*, only the need to find words, syntax, structure and meter for feelings that do not go into words.

Emotions have no definition other than themselves. They are irreducible, the atoms of sensation. All written art is an attempt to communicate what it is to feel, to ask the terrifying question: Is what I experience in my head the same as what you experience? Terrifying because we can never know for certain. We hope; we risk.

My hopeful, fearful little English heart is in smithereens.

I know who you are now. The Receiver Block women are superlative gossips. *New men on the base.* Ben Seligman. A man in white, a boffin. A doctor of physics, from Caius College, Cambridge, but your people are from Manchester, generations deep. I hear only the northern richness of your accent as I pass Boffins Corner: Ruby, another Lancastrian, pinpointed your accent. You've never spoken to me in it. But you've looked, and you look and we catch each other's eyes and hold for that safe moment.

I think it's a kind of radar. You can't see it, can't hear it; it doesn't touch any of our senses and all it returns are ghosts, but from those ghosts we can work out a heading, an orientation.

Autumn arrived in tumbled weather fronts and a sense of meteorological safety: no invasion this season. I migrated indoors. In Poets Corner I hide behind my beer and plan a hundred love poems to you, none of which I dare ever publish, none of which I can ever complete.

And I look up and you are there in front of me, your face awkward, your feet clumsy, and you set the pint in front of me.

"Do you take bribes?"

Oh God say something shape words utter coherencies. I smile and nod.

"You're Tom Chappell, aren't you?"

"I am."

"Tom the Rhymer."

I hear him capitalize it. It's gone quiet in the Receiver Block snug.

I make a stupid apologetic half smile, half dip of the head.

He extends a hand.

"Ben Seligman."

I know that.

His hand is hot. Nerves. Mine is admirably cool from the pint.

"I was wondering. I've got myself involved in the base pantomime. I know, I didn't move quickly enough. I'm running the lights, but I need someone to help with the other technical stuff; sound effects, rigging, all that. I hear you know a bit about it."

I know no such things.

"If you've got the time, I'd appreciate a hand."

Our eyes touch.

"Yes," I say. "Happy to oblige."

And he smiles and bites back the smile for fear of it shining too bright, and clumsily, apologetically, awkwardly he makes his way back to Boffins Corner. He nods to me again and smiles as they rise from their table to make their beery way back to base: he has an excuse now.

I wait for the radar girls to pile from the back room in a pall of cigarette smoke.

"Lizzie."

She hangs back in the doorway.

"Did you tell him I knew about stage lighting?"

"I thought you did," she says. "Sorry if I got you into trouble. You can always tell him no."

"It would be a shame to let him down."

"It would that."

~

He blows me during Nurse Bedpan's "Oh no, he isn't; oh yes, he is" routine. Captain McTavish is out on the stage in the full Grande Dame wig and pancake makeup, batting banter and badinage back and forth with the front rows. I'm on the follow spot keeping him lit while in the shadows the stage crew dress the set for the Robin Hood Silver Arrow Scene when I first feel arms around my waist, then the movement of a hand down, and an unzip and a hand cupping me, then a tongue working its magic.

I manage to whisper a protest about the danger the danger, but he takes his lips away for a moment to whisper back, "No one will see. They're blind in this light."

The lighting gantry in Bawdsey Village Hall is the size

of a large wardrobe, the heat from the rheostats like a blast furnace, put a hand wrong you electrocute yourself and directly beneath my feet Robin Hood and his Merry Men are waiting for the cue from the stage manager and Ben is blowing me brilliantly, beautifully, dirtily. Evil evil boy: if I waver, if the spot drifts for an instant, Captain McTavish will have me on jankers for a week. Two hundred kids, evacuees, locals, RAF and the clergy of St. Mary's roar with laughter to the Dame as Ben finishes me by hand, wipes me off, does me up and is up at the rheostats to light the entrance of the singing, prancing Merry Men.

There are five curtain calls. All in all, opening night of RAF Bawdsey's panto *Babes in the Wood* is a thundering success.

Lambeth

I saw her come down the platform towards the barrier and started waving. There is something about London mainline stations that makes all partings and meetings cinematic. She grinned broadly. I had never seen her smile before.

I took her backpack and we went to drop her stuff off at the Premier Inn. I fidgeted in the lobby while Thorn took an age to settle herself. I was excited that Thorn had come up to London. She hadn't been in London for fifteen years. There was so much I wanted to show her. I was excited about our appointment with Shahrzad at the Imperial War Museum. I had e-mailed her my photographs and then assumed she had forgotten about them. Since I first met her at the acquittal party following a literary forgery case and seen her extraordinary abilities, I have called on her talents occasionally and learned to work with her timetable and calendar, or not at all. When Shahrzad e-mailed me five days later to let me know she had something interesting, I knew it was more than just that.

The Imperial War Museum was a ten-minute walk across Geraldine Mary Harmsworth Park to the All Saints Annexe where the photographic collection was stored.

"So, you said talent?" Thorn asked. Her hands were thrust deep in pockets, her scarf pulled tight. The park was layered and fragrant with late autumn leaves, swept into crisp drifts by a stiffening westerly wind. Voices called from the soccer pitches for the ball, for a pass.

"Shahrzad is a super-recognizer," I said. "Pretty useful for a photo archivist. Most of them work for the police. They can spot someone in CCTV footage and remember that they've seen that face before, even if it was years ago, and where and when. The Met's asked her to work for them, but she doesn't view the police as friends. Her family escaped from Iran in 1979 and there was always someone watching, either the police or the Iranian Embassy. But you must *never* call her Iranian. She's Persian."

We left coats and bags and picked up our passes.

"It's 'Hildreth' with an e, not 'Hildrith' with an i," Thorn hissed as the intern took us up to the viewing room.

Shahrzad was late. Shahrzad was early by Shahrzad time. Just as I was about to text her the door burst open and a short, solid woman in her midforties stormed into the Visitors' Room in a flurry of scarves and sleeves. She banged boxes and files and her handbag down on the table. Her face was a mask of fury.

"Fucking Charlie Greenall. Fucking middle-micro-wank-management. Fucking team meetings. What the fuck gets done in meetings anyway? How are you, Emmett?" Her face lit up like sun breaking through a storm. Shahrzad was one of those people whose natural demeanor is naturally glowering but whose smile, rare and always earned, was radiant as a saint. Before I could answer, she said, "You must be Thorn, yes?" Her handshake was as intimidating as her countenance. Thorn did not wince, though I saw bones shift under her skin. "Thirtieth letter of the Icelandic alphabet." She spread her folders out on the table and we sat.

"Thank you for sending this to me, Emmett. It entertained me greatly." She turned her heavily mascaraed eyes on Thorn and her face settled into storm again. "Have you thought of donating all this stuff to us? Rural attics, darling, no. Rats, mice. Pigeon shit. Fire. Flood. Darling, in ten years' time, when climate change has wreaked its fearful work upon us, the North Sea's going to run as far as fucking Cambridge. Your little plastic boxes will be bobbing, darling. Bobbing. The amount of priceless material that gets ruined by well-intentioned amateurs: Have you any idea the damage something as simple as seasonal temperature variations is doing to your great-grandfather's archive? Of course you don't. You need the Seven Ps. Professional Paper Preservation Protects Perfect Precious Pictures. Photographs are like children, sweetie. You care for them, you nurture them, you love, but one day, well, you just have to let them go.

"Now, the material." She laid out printouts of the documents I had sent her. "Emmett, your letter. Pretty boys have a lovely time in Alexandria. It's wartime, everyone's at it like knives, seen it before. Thorn, your great-grandfather is as nasty a little bigoted shit as I never care to meet again. This, however." She tapped the photographs at the pyramids. "This I can work with. This exercises my grey matter. I see this and I think, 'Hello, boys, I know you from somewhere, don't I?' And it transpires that I did."

She slipped a printout, facedown, from a folder and turned it up. A country pub, red tiled, low windowed; a cart, shafts up; arranged against it, soldier boys. Arms folded, leaning nonchalantly, looking into the camera. Battle dress open at the collar, necks burned from the plowing, puttees neatly wound around farm-boy calves. No weapons, no hats, no identifying badges, moustached all. First World War recruits before the embarkation, an image from a murdered England. Boys, friends all. I could see that from their easy familiarity: Here were young men who had grown up together. A pals regiment.

"Here." I spotted them the instant before Shahrzad's finger descended. The dark-haired man with his arm around the towheaded man's shoulder, each of them looking into the lens with an expression deeper than pride and adventure. Here were knowing, experience, dread. Thorn let out a small gasp of wonder.

"The picture was taken on the twenty-eighth of July 1915," Shahrzad said. "The pub is The Rose and Crown, Snettisham."

"Snettisham, that's near . . . ," I said.

"Sandringham."

"The Sandringham Pals," I said.

"Sorry?" Thorn said.

"Lord Kitchener's war strategy was based on a constant stream of fresh bodies to overwhelm the enemy," Shahrzad said. "Conscription was an alien notion in the British army, which had always been professional; so to sugar the pill, groups that enlisted in the same place served together. Pals battalions. There were works battalions, three football team battalions, even a Stockbrokers' Battalion. The Sandringham Pals were all workers on the royal estate."

"The Fifth Norfolks," I said. "The Vanished Regiment."

Shahrzad nodded.

"Explain?" Thorn asked.

"Two days later the Sandringham Pals were amalgamated into the Fifth Norfolk Regiment and shipped out from Liverpool to the Dardanelles. The Fifth Norfolks were part of the Hundred-and-Sixty-Third Brigade—here's how it works, sweetie. Very roughly: One hundred men, a battalion. One thousand men, a regiment. Two thousand men, a brigade. Ten thousand men, a division. They landed at Suvla Bay on August tenth. Two days later the One-Hundred-and-Sixty-Third was sent into action to dislodge Turkish positions on the Anafarta Plain. They marched into sheer fucking hell. They were criminally under-prepared. They were over-dressed for the heat of Turkey in August. They had rubbish arms, poor provisions, and they were ordered to advance in broad daylight into well-prepared Ottoman defenses, dug in deep on the Kavak Tepe hill. They managed to push the Ottomans back into a forest set ablaze by artillery fire. They advanced up into the smoke and flame and that was the last anyone ever saw of them, disappearing into the smoke. The Vanished Battalion."

"God," Thorn said. "What happened?"

"The archaeology suggests a massacre," Shahrzad said. "The Ottomans executed all their prisoners."

"There is another theory," I ventured.

"The MJ-Twelve account is nonsense," Shahrzad said with heat.

"The New Zealand Army Corps signed sworn statements that they had seen six to eight lenticular-shaped clouds over Kavak Tepe," I said.

"Reichardt didn't come forward with that account until 1965," Shahrzad said. She slipped photocopies out of another folder. "And he says that no explanation can be found in the historical records of the Imperial War Museum's archives. Shahrzad Hejazi says there's a lot more in the archives than we're telling, sweetie. This stays in the building. And if I ever hear whisper of this, Emmett Leigh, you will end your days selling blow jobs to bookdealers." One piece of paper, facedown of course, to Thorn, one to me. "This is what the Anzacs really saw. Now, milk in coffee? Sugar?"

August 11th

My dearest Mamaji,

A few short lines, written in fierce haste, for soon I shall see action again and with my whole heart I dread it.

I have been posted away from the Australians, for which I was at first grateful, for, as you know from my previous letters, I found their customary roughness, their excessive mannishness, uncongenial. I have been seconded to an English brigade, where I will be serving not with my brother muleteers, but as a stretcher-bearer, which suits my disposition and spiritual demeanour better. Mamaji: these English! We are taught to consider them our betters, but whereas the Australians accepted me as a man, if effete by their lights, these Anglians do not see me as human at all. I will not offend your sensibilities, my dear Mama, with the names and sobriquets they afflict on me.

I have met a few agreeable types. There is a corporal, quite ill, a brother poet. We have agreed to read and critique each other's work. I wonder if he realises what he has let himself in for! Fortunate for him that I have not written a word since shipping out from Egypt, else the pile of papers would be insurmountable. Urdu is everywhere acknowledged the true language of poetry, and yet I find the words elude me; they slip from the folds of mind even as the image is formed. Mute visions. I am dry of poetry. The corporal's work is passable, if leaden, in both weight and lustre, and I struggle to bring myself to read it.

The corporal has a close friend, dark as he is fair. Both of them are oddities among the dull yeomanry of the Sandringhams. Everything about them is out of place: their accents, their breadth of experience, *their age—these are mature men, leading eager, dull boys—their worldliness. I would call them old souls. You say I have an eye for where the worlds met, Ma-maji: these two men, inseparable friends, seem to me to have rinsed through many lives, many turns. The other ranks seem to believe that if they are with them, they are somehow protected. They are admirable company, fine conversationalists and well schooled in the sciences and the arts, though not, alas, in the mag-nificent culture and history of my own land. We share tea and poetry—the corporal carries a small volume of verse next to his heart—and listen to the guns. The eternal guns.*

Those guns were busy again this night. There is to be a push. There is always a push, and a push back, and again a push forward: a few footsteps over these hillsides veined with trenches, so close we can smell the Turkish cigarettes. The trenches talk of glory, but all I see is breakage and the waste. I carry it back to the lines on my stretcher.

Your devoted son,
Amal

~

August 12th

My dearest Mamaji,

I trust this finds you, and yet I trust that it does not. Post has been suspended, so I have secreted my letters to you, my fragrant mother, in my pocket book in the hope that, should the worst befall, they might find you with my other personal effects.

With first light the guns fell silent. Soon the whistles would sound and trenches give up their bodies like an obscene parody of the Christian resurrection. I had just shared a light with my two friends, Seligman and Chappell, when we heard a new sound. Not the guns, not their echo across that blasted hillside, something new and otherworldly. The best I can describe, it was like one of the dry season storms that rolls in from the Deccan, that the old Sufis call the Hammer of God. The stuff of legends and childhood terrors.

At once Seligman and Chappell left off their smoke with me. They pushed a periscope up over the top of the trench, then, without so much as a word, they put up a scaling ladder and ran up it, Seligman leading Chappell by the hand like a mother leading a child to the well. It was as if, deep in that strange thunder, something had spoken their names. By now the battalion was awake and wide-eyed with alarm, but before anyone could stop them they were into No Man's Land.

As one we rushed to the parapet. We looked into fiery hell, such as the Christians and Buddhists relish: a ball of darkness, flickering with light, like lightning tied in a knot. Silhouetted against this blazing backdrop, the crouching figures of Seligman and Chappell hastened from shell hole to shell hole, trench to abandoned trench, as the Ottomans opened up.

"At them, lads!" our officers cried, and we returned fire, but ineffectually and with bafflement, for we saw that as my friends moved towards the storm, it moved towards them. A hot wind blew in our faces. I thought I imagined strange voices on it: cries, implorings, laughter, and saw from the faces of the soldiers that I was not alone.

Seligman and Chappell ran towards this cloud. Our Lieutenant shouted their names, twice, reached for his service revolver, then snapped the holster shut on it again. I saw the cloud open to receive them. I saw the lightning part, and them go up into it, hand in hand like children. Then the cloud closed and the thunder ceased and the hot wind and the things that spoke in it fell still. Before our astonished eyes, the cloud vanished into itself. Folded inwards, and was gone, and Seligman and Chappell with it.

Why, in the midst of such immense horror, in the middle of a push, do I dwell on this strange incident? Perhaps because it is an indicative madness, the insanity that reveals the greater insanity. Everything we know and trust is broken here; we deal in outrages, so is it so strange if nature outrages itself, and us?

Moments after, the whistles blew. Dawn had come, and we must rise and fight. Did we dream what we saw? Was it a collective nightmare, forged in the insanity of war? The whistles sounded; with a cheer the Sandringham Pals rose up and went over the top. And I sat, awaiting my call to go and bring what remains of them back, writing to you, my dearest Mamaji.

They are crying now: "Bearers! Bearers!" Stretcher parties.

I must sign this letter now, Mamaji, and place it for safekeeping. My love to my dear sisters.

Your devoted son,
Amal

~

After the museum, I suggested a drink. Thorn had an app, a beer app, for real beer. It directed us to a tiny drinkery the size of two armchairs pushed together. We fitted into a booth like segments of orange into its skin and she ordered. The app gave her trophies and rewards for new pubs, new beers, local specialities, potable Pokémons.

Thorn was still wide-eyed from Shahrzad's secrets, served with bad coffee and chocolate Hobnobs. Shahrzad had repeated her promises of dark retribution as she packed away the material and escorted us to the elevators, but I knew as well as she that these were for Thorn's benefit: one scanty account, from a battalion without survivors, was evidence that only conspiracists would accept. The Sandringham Pals had marched into massacre. The fates of two seeming deserters were irrelevant.

A photographer captured them outside a Norfolk pub. They ran up into the cloud of mystery. Twenty-four years later another photographer captured them in front of the Sphinx.

In the Sandringham photograph, they had been older than their chums. Late twenties, early thirties. In the Giza picture, they must have been at least in their midforties. We put the pictures side by side. There was hardly a day between them.

"There's something nagging me," Shahrzad had said as the elevator doors closed, her *esprit de l'escalier*. "I never forget a face. It's a professional pride thing."

"Abductees!" Thorn said with luminous excitement.

We were on our second pints by them. "What Amal was describing, that's a classic abduction scenario."

"In the middle of the Gallipoli campaign?"

"War is a great time to abduct. People go missing all the time. Do you want to go on somewhere else?"

~

"All mystical experiences could be abductions," Thorn said as her app led us to the next pub, a painstakingly de-decorated arch under Waterloo East where the frowns of the cool staff and drinkers relegated us to the back table in the farthest room. "Angel visitations, fairy hills, Moses on Sinai. Any sufficiently advanced technology is indistinguishable from magic."

"Arthur C. Clarke," I said. "I read him a lot when I was a kid, I read a lot of SF, but I drifted away. I'm sort of a lapsed Catholic. But if you're talking ancient aliens and all that stuff, you'd be surprised the money you can get for early-edition Erich von Dänikens. *The Morning of the Magicians* too. Some dealers specialize in esoterica."

The staff turned the music up to get rid of us.

"Everyone has a camera on their phone and no one sees UFOs anymore," I said.

"'But you have to admit, Emmett," Thorn said, her breath steaming, her beanie hat pulled down over her ears, "it's a mystery."

We wandered the South Bank as the sun threw long shadows across the raw concrete of the Queen Elizabeth II Centre. Skateboarders rumbled and clacked in their brutalist undercroft. I admire the resilience of a sport that is 90 percent failure. That evening the sky was vast and the city, awaking in lights, amenable and tender. Even the runners were smiling. We agreed that the app was excellent and true, but its virtue was effort and we settled for the best available in each of the riverfront cafes and bars. By the time we reached Doggett's Coat and Badge we were six pints gone and the starlings were swirling out from under Blackfriars Bridge into the indigo sky and watching their ever-changing swirling and flocking—a meta-living thing—I thought that all the mystery we need surrounds us at every moment in a cloud of wonders, small and great and only manifest when we look at them.

But I was quite drunk then, and 70 percent in love, I reckon.

I walked Thorn back to her hotel—she didn't invite me in, though she hesitated—and then back, electrically connected to everything in the universe, to Clapham.

~

Shahrzad woke me.

I get so few calls I'd forgotten my ring tone. I surfaced noisily, groggily, through my piles of duvets and quilts and slapped around until my hand hit glass.

"What the hell time is it?"

"Two o'clock, sweetie. Some of us do our best work in the morning." Shahrzad time, of course. But only two days since I had seen Thorn off on her train to the Fens. "Sent you a something. I knew it, I knew I knew it."

"Couldn't you just have . . . ," I began but Shahrzad had already rung off. *Texted.* No sweetie, no texts: itty-bitty fiddly stuff. For kids to pass notes in school. She couldn't just send something. She had to ring to tell me she'd sent something.

I opened the attachment.

I studied the image until my eyes itched.

Then I called Thorn.

~

I met Thorn at King's Cross and whisked her to the near-est decent pub her app could identify. It did not have snugs, but I insisted Thorn find the quietest, most remote table and waited for the small talk to subside before lay-ing out my print of what Shahrzad had found between the pints of double-hopped IPA.

"That's a modern-looking tank," Thorn said. "Blue

helmets . . . Where is this?"

"Bosnia. Somewhere outside the village Goritsa."

"Goritsa? Why do I know that name?"

"There was a massacre. A Bosnian Serb warlord called Vlatko Vicic. He's doing life in the Hague. This is the UNPROFOR unit after it had been ordered to abandon Goritsa."

"Some heroes," Thorn said.

"The picture is a screen grab from an old Channel Four documentary called *Ten Days in the Death of Goritsa*." I rested a finger on the print. "Look."

It took Thorn a few seconds to see what I had seen. Shahrzad had seen then immediately, remembered then from a fleeting viewing a year before.

"My God," Thorn breathed.

The image was blurry and low def, snatched from a copy of a copy of a VHS tape. Three Warrior APCs were parked up at an overlook on a winding mountain road. The sky was clear, the sun brilliant, the day glorious and the vista of forested mountains and abrupt, plunging valleys heartbreaking. All the squaddies had their sleeves rolled up and wore shades and shapeless fishing hats to keep the sun from their English skins. Tea break.

Of course.

I couldn't tell if this photograph was taken before the UNPROFOR force arrived or after it was ordered to abandon the village to the Butcher of Goritsa.

But they weren't alone. In the background were the documentary crew's vehicles, a tractor and trailer, a small country bus and a couple of UN ancillary vehicles. People looked out at the view or sat on the parapet. Smiling at the camera, almost recognizable under aviator shades and those same God-ugly hats: Seligman and Chappell.

Not unrecognizable to a talent like Shahrzad.

"When was this taken?" Thorn breathed.

"Nineteen-ninety-five."

"That would make them . . ."

"At the very youngest, one hundred and five years old." A shiver ran through me, chilling but delicious at the same time, the frisson of human reason running into the impossible yet undeniable.

"I was wrong," Thorn whispered and I could hear the same awed tremble in her voice. ' "Not abductees. *Immortals*."

~

Ten Days in the Death of Goritsa had gone out late on a minority channel, been well reviewed in the broadsheet press and vanished, as had the production company that made it. I tracked down the director and persuaded her to meet us for lunch at a wine bar in Soho close to the post-production house where she was cutting a new film about child soldiers in Southern Sudan.

I think she was disappointed that we weren't offering her work.

She frowned at the pictures in the printout, then called up the film on her MacBook. We crowded around the screen, straining to make out the voices from the tinny speakers. Chappell and Seligman were on-screen for thirty seconds. Seligman smiled. Chappell spoke three lines. The film cut to the armored convoy driving off.

"Do you remember anything about them?" I asked.

She remembered the curiosity of two Englishmen in the middle of the bloody collapse of Yugoslavia, without any obvious connections or affiliations or mission.

"Everyone thought they were spies," the director said. "Then again, they thought we were spies. Some side's useful idiots."

I pressed her for more details, but her head was full of South Sudanese boy soldiers and burning villages.

"They were trying to get to Belgrade and then on to Budapest," she said. "I hope they made it. It was a hideous time. Anything could get you killed."

She looked pointedly at the time on her phone. I thanked her and got the lunch bill. She gave me a DVD.

Shingle Street

I know Shingle Street in high summer sun, when sky, sea and stone are metal beneath its hammer; when the stones burn the bare foot, and I now know Shingle Street as the sun leaves and everything hangs, between moments, between worlds. These are the stolen moments.

As a boffin—the Uncertainty Squad, they called themselves, a white-coated coven in their little, separate cottage hung heavy with power cables—Ben has unquestioned access to the key to the Martello tower. He brings the key; I bring the motorbike. Wind in our hair as we ride up the beach.

I'm glad the leave didn't work out as planned. I would have felt uncomfortable going up to Manchester with Ben, back to his friends and family. London would have been just more people and what we want is unpeople. Time and space for us.

We set up home quickly and lightly, with a thrill of shaping our own unregulated space. I lie naked on the grass before the Martello tower drinking sun while Ben negotiates the Primus stove and Tilley lamp. We eat soft-boiled eggs in the glow of burning paraffin and sun-burned skin flakes from my too-Saxon flesh. The evening is immense, endless; the dawns, unfolding imperceptibly from the sea, overpowering. There is no need for words.

Endless summer, for two days.

The unsubstantiated rumors of the east wind in the tough, spiny grass.

The soft lop of the pebbles on a barely perceptible swell, day and night.

The long vapor trails of the high bombers, the curlicues of the Hurricanes sent to intercept. War poems written on the sky.

The low, lean strokes of warships, seeming to hover on the silver lines of heat haze along the horizon.

The stillness, the emptiness of the evacuated hamlet.

Nights in each other's arms.

~

When heaven and earth and stone are in equilibrium, the slightest change will send ripples. I wake. Instantly, I know why. Ben is gone. I roll out of my bivvy bag and pad down the spiral staircase in my skin. The door is open. The night is fast and crystalline, each star a stress point where a new universe might break through. A glow from around the curve of the tower. Ben sits reading in the glow of the Tilley lamp. He moves; the light shifts; I recognize the set of the words, the formalism of the space on the page. He is reading my book.

And I am ablaze with jealousy.

I watch him flip the pages with a finger, a casual whip, no more than a glance at each poem. I can't bear the thought of him carelessly tearing a page.

"Ben," I say. I might have shot him, so sudden and extreme is his shock. My jealousy dispels.

Ben sets the book down, puts his hands up.

"Mea culpa."

"You could have asked."

"Mea maxima culpa."

I slide in beside him.

"Are you not a bit cold?" he asks.

I shake my head. "It's natural."

"It's just, well, Cheetham Hill boys don't run around in the buff."

"Can I have my book back?" I ask.

He hands it to me, eyes down-turned in guilt.

"I wanted to see what it was about," Ben says. "I didn't want you to see how I reacted. In case I didn't like it."

"How do you react?"

"I don't have a poet's soul."

High, I hear the throb of bomber engines. It's the dark of the moon, the sky the bomber pilots hate and hope for, when they can neither see nor be seen. The anti-aircraft batteries at Lowestoft begin, soft cracks building into a symphony. Behind the Martello tower the western sky will be alive with lights.

"Who was he?" Ben asks.

"A traveler. A man on a beach. He'd be here, about where you're sitting. When I had to get out, just go somewhere, away from school, away from the village and the church and everyone wanting something from me, he'd be here. And we'd talk. Sometimes we'd go up the beach up to Orford Ness; sometimes, if the weather was good, we'd just sit here. You can't be seen from the houses here. It's a hidden place. Hours would pass. I'd get back home and my mam would say, 'Where were you until this hour?' and I'd say, 'Just out, walking.' I didn't want to tell her about him. I knew what she'd say. It was never like that."

"What did you talk about?"

"You'll laugh."

"I would never laugh at you."

"Poems. Poetry. Poets. Books. Words, how strong they are, how agile and easy to escape, how they never quite tell the thing as it is. Language and how close it comes to truth, and how far away it is. What it can say and what it can't say. Feeling: its irreducibility, how it can't be broken down into any simpler or more explicable. Do you know what I'm saying?"

"I'm trying to."

"He did. I told him things I couldn't tell anyone else. Try talking in school about wanting to write poetry. Let alone anything . . . you know."

"I shouldn't have read your book."

"He gave me the book the day before he left. He always said he couldn't stay for long. I never heard from him again. But the book—this book—every poem, spoke to me. Every poem felt as if it had been written just for me. Everything I thought and felt and doubted but knew deep down, it was there. It's not great poetry. It's terrible poetry. But it's my poetry. There was a thing he always said, after we said good-bye. He would wait here and I would go back down Shingle Street, and he would always look out to sea and say, 'Storm's coming.' Even on the clearest days. I think I know what he meant, now."

"The war."

I lean close to Ben, for I'm cold now, and self-conscious.

"War brought you," I say.

He leans his cheek against my head. A quick peck. The east is lightening, a line of bruise yellow along the horizon.

"Weather's on the change," I say.

The anti-aircraft guns have stopped. Bomber engines

pulse overhead, beating back to the Low Countries.

~

In two hours we return to Bawdsey. I don't want it to end. It will end. Everything good comes to an end. Pack up the bivvy bags and the camp beds, stow away the stove and the lamp. Load the motorbike and bury the rubbish.

He hops up behind he, locks his arms around my waist. I kick the engine; she starts like she always starts, true and beautiful thing. My weather sense was true: storm's coming. I gun the bike up Shingle Street towards the radar masts of Bawdsey as the first fat drops burst on the sun-dry stones and the Dutch horizon crawls with lightning.

Fenland

There was no one point at which I could be certain that *after this I lived with Thorn Hildreth*. Points there were: That first visit. That night she invited me to sleep over on the sofa. *You will wake up with a dog,* she warned. Not one but three: the German shepherd/collie cross at my feet; the collie/spaniel cross between me and the back of the sofa, threatening to spill me onto the cigarette-burned carpet; and the Jack Russell in my right armpit. That breakfast when I asked, *You've got plenty of space in the barn; would you mind if I stored a few boxes of books here?* The afternoon I graduated from the sofa in the Thunor Study to the Frig bedroom: each room in the long, rambling house—added to longitudinally by each generation of Hildreths so that one end was collapsing even as the other was a barely begun construction site—was named after a member of Leland Hildreth's Hilderwic pantheon. The January morning when I looked out across the frost-sharp fields to the line of misted poplars and found the prospect not familiar but heart tugging. When I stopped smelling her patchouli from every furnishing and surface, realizing when I smelled it again that it was coming from my own skin.

Points that map a curve.

Hirne House, the manor of the Hildreths, was big enough to hold many lives and histories. Leland thumped around as if in a state of quantum superposition, not quite in the kitchen or the living room, not quite not. He never spoke to me, though he seemed aware of my existence. His greatest obsession was worrying whether the antique wiring would decide one night to burn us in our beds or the Doverhirne Drain would rise and sweep us all into the Wash. Thorn survived in the fashion of the New Rural: a job here, a gig there: part-time classroom assistant, helper at the local animal welfare center (the dogs, the cats, the ponies, donkey and chinchillas), charity shop worker, occasional manager for the local metal band—Elder Würm—bespoke motorbike repairs and, latterly, packing and shipping rare books from my two-by-four-and-fiberboard office in her cold but dry barn.

Moving the books that had imprisoned me in my two hideous rooms in Clapham turned out not to be such a Sisyphean task. I came back from my first stay to London and saw a city I recognized but no longer loved. I saw London grown cold, self-obsessed, arrogant. I saw the anti-street-sleeper spikes, the posh and pov doors to the same apartment blocks, the curtain walls of empty gold-brick houses defending wealth and unearned income. London, pre-eminently the city of literature, had turned away from books.

What I could not dispose of in a mass sale to my bibliophile friends went into the back of Elder Würm's Transit. I squeezed in the front between the vocalist and the bass player, accompanied up the A1M by their Death Metal Drive Mix. The same metal friends occasionally laid a few courses of bricks or set in a joist or door lintel in the new extension to Hirne House.

Dealerdom and those few bookstore owners who hadn't barred me for serial Wi-Fi abuse held a wake for me in a terrible pub in Bloomsbury trading long on overdrawn literary associations and short on charisma. Thorn's app would have shown us somewhere better. Thorn was absent. I didn't want my book colleagues to meet her.

"It's not like I'm dead," I said. "It's only Lincolnshire."

"Better death than Lincolnshire," Louisa in Louboutins intoned.

"They have bookstores in King's Lynn," I insisted.

"They have line dancing in King's Lynn," Tall Lionel reminded me. "And motor sport."

I couldn't deny the motor sport.

Shahrzad sent halva and hugs over the phone. *Love*

to be there, sweetie, but I'm at a conference in Madrid with Fucking Charlie Greenall. How had that story panned out anyway? Deliciously?

The Goritsa fragment had thrilled and frozen us. It was as if we had opened a drawer of our parents' secrets and now we feared that what we had seen would break all our familiar delusions. *Immortals*, Thorn had whispered. Craziness. But how else could we explain what we had seen? We drew back; we folded the secrets and closed the drawer. What if we had caught the gaze of beings—powers—beyond our comprehension? Glamour is danger.

But glamour attracts, and one night at the death of the old year, with the wind whipping sleet in from the North Sea and bending the poplars to the ground, we took a bottle to the wood-burning stove and gazed into the glamour. Leland was wind-crazy, clacking around the house with his stick, unable to settle, as if his private gods were circling above him. Hirne House creaked and cracked. The plastic sheeting covering the new build flapped and rattled. In the morning we would find it shredded across fifteen miles of hedgerow and barbed-wire fence.

"Immortals," Thorn said. She poured supermarket port. "Like *Highlander*. An ancient order of immortals, careful of their secrets, hidden from history."

"If I were an immortal, the last place I would put myself is the middle of the biggest wars in history," I said.

Thorn kicked off her boots and curled up beside me on the collapsing leather sofa.

"So? You're immortal."

"So a seventy-five-millimeter artillery round scores a direct hit and you walk away not a hair out of place?" I said. "That's not immortal; that's indestructible. *Captain Scarlet,* not *Highlander*."

"Immortal is, you cannot die."

"Immortal is, you live forever, unless something kills you. Indestructible breaks the laws of physics. Thermodynamics, even before you get to biology. Indestructible is magic. It's miracles in the real world. It's like moving statues and weeping Madonnas and the sun standing still at Fatima. It breaks everything. That's not the world we can exist in."

"Yet there they were."

"I can believe in beings with incredibly long lives. But they can die. Seventy-five-millimeter artillery shells can kill them as quickly and completely as you or I. Amortal, I suppose."

"Can't have amortal. It's already taken. It means never really living in the first place. It's from Harry Potter."

"Emortal, then. I read that in an old SF book. How old did they look in the Bosnian War picture?"

"Late thirties," Thorn said. I had no eye for the sub-
tleties of the Seven Ages. People were young until they
were middle-aged until they were senior. "In the Sandringham picture, I'd say midtwenties at the most."

"We can work this out," I said, and while Thorn
shooed the shepherd-collie away from the bottle of port
glowing in the firelight I hauled an old bank statement
from the unopened pile on the coffee table and ran a
few numbers in the margin. "So, say they age an apparent
twelve years between 1915 and 1995. That's a ratio of six-
point-six years of ours to one of theirs."

"Like dog years." Thorn ruffled the shepherd-collie's
ear with her foot. "So, if they were late twenties in
1899 . . ."

"They were born sometime in the seventeen seven-
ties," I said, and felt cold steal in from the dying part of
the house and caress my spine.

"And they're still out there," Thorn said in a suddenly
small voice.

I imagined the emortals, always among us, always
apart, ever wary of the mortal host that if it ever learned
of their existence would stop at nothing to tear their secrets from them.

And if they were discovered, what would they do to re-
gain their anonymity? I shivered again, despite the enor-
mous heat glowing from the cast-iron stove. Dogs stirred

and groaned, weakly thumping tails in the expectation of a run outside, collapsing in a sigh onto the rug when they heard the sleet pelt the ill-fitting windows.

"Do you want another bottle of port?" Thorn said.

"Oh, go on."

The dogs looked up as Thorn went into the ramshackle kitchen. I heard a cork squeak.

"Leland has a stash," Thorn said, returning with a dusty bottle. "Anson laid it down for him. He'll never drink it all. It could be a bit sedimenty."

"Pass me the laptop. I'd like another look at that documentary."

"You've already seen it ten times," Thorn complained, but handed it over. I opened the player and turned down the volume. "What are you looking for?"

A thing I might have glimpsed and forgotten, a detail the camera might inadvertently have captured, a clue that might lead us forward from this seeming dead stop on a mountain road in Bosnia. Shahrzad's gift is to recognize and remember. My gift is smaller and less flashy: I *notice*. I stabbed a finger at the screen.

"There."

Thorn leaned in until her face almost touched the screen. Blue lit, ambient with port and patchouli.

"What?"

"That little speck on the parapet. Next to Chappell."

"That's their lunch."

"Can you zoom this thing in?"

"Like *Blade Runner*? Enhance thirty-four to forty-six?"

"Just show me how to do it."

"You unpinch. Like this."

The resolution was dire, almost as bad as the screen-grab, but my talent had led me true. I stretched the image to its limits, a tiny square of color, a handful of pixels. A fleck of color. I increased the color saturation. Green. Green as God's eyes.

"The book," I said. "I found the letter in it; the Gallipoli letters mentioned it. That's the book. *Time Was*."

"And?" Thorn poured more time-dark port.

"I think if you find the book, you find them."

A door creaked open. Sudden wind, free in the house, made the fire flare up. The dogs roused, eyes wide. The door slammed. We sat paralyzed with fear; then Thorn leapt to her feet.

"Fucking Leland!" She rushed in her stocking feet to the front door. "He's only gone outside to check the level in the Drain!"

It took her fifteen minutes to haul Leland, barefoot in his dressing gown, back from the treacherous edge of the river into the house, get him into bed, tranquilize him with whisky. By the time she made it back wet-footed to the port the fire had died down to embers, the dogs gone, the room cooling, and the ghosts, gods and immortals we had summoned had dissolved back into wind.

"The Frig bedroom has terrible draughts, Emmett," Thorn said.

I thought of telling her about the new leak, inscribing a black powdery fungus stain into the exterior corner of the wall, but I had a hope of where this was going.

"And that shit three-bar heater. The Othun bedroom, however, is draft-free, centrally heated, and can offer the additional comfort of my fine warm ass."

She got up, careful to show me that ass in her thread-bare Adidas leggings.

"I'll bring the bottle. You bring the glasses."

~

Thorn had to apply for a passport. I found it aston-ishing that a modern woman had never been outside the UK. I fretted through the tedious process of form filling and submitting photographs and finding some-one respectable to authenticate the photographs—I offered, as a respectable entrepreneur in the used-book trade, but she went for the vicar—and having the thing couriered back to her. I fidgeted that every delay meant that the book might be gone—I'd e-mailed, I'd even called, but from the replies it was clear that my execrable French had dropped into a Manche of miscommunication. I think the shop had reserved it, but at every instant I feared someone walking out with it in a nicely printed canvas bookstore bag.

La Sauterelle was a maze of rooms on five different floors around a courtyard off the Rue des Saints-Pères. It smelled of coffee, cat piss, must and stale perfume. It smelled of Thorn's world, I realized.

It took me twenty minutes to find *Time Was*. The buyer who bought it from me had been an agent. Not for secret immortals, but for a Left Bank bookstore specializing in the arcane, the hard to get, the unique. I e-mailed La Sauterelle, booked train tickets and fretted for a week while Thorn got a passport.

La Sauterelle was created to caress my bibliophile nerve endings. Eccentric architecture. Stacks in corridors, staircases lined with books so you had to side-wind up them, cautious of triggering a paper avalanche; rooms connected like synapses. Idiosyncratic cataloguing: by jacket color rather than subject, by poetic theme, by the geographical location of the author. An entire room was dedicated to pastry-cooking. I knew I could lose hours—ideally days—in this paper labyrinth. Our train left Gare du Nord at 21:13.

The store had reserved it for me. "They are much sought after," the woman at the Belle Epoque table that was the cash desk told me. "The owner has instructions."

"Instructions?"

"They are quite old. From the earliest days of the store. They are passed down, generation to generation. It is a special book."

"How old is the store?"

"One hundred and twenty-five years next July."

I picked up the book. I felt its heft, the grain of its cover, the slight tear of ragged edges of the bound signatures. I opened it, sniffed the pages. Fusty, still damp from the dumpster where I had found it months before, outside the corpse of The Golden Page. Not the smell of a 125-year-old book.

"I sold this copy to one of your book-finders. I found it outside an old bookstore in London."

"I understand there are others."

"Bookstores with . . . instructions?"

"Part of the instructions are that, should one of those stores close, the book is to go to another. The London store had clearly forgotten their instructions."

"You have another copy?"

"Of course we do."

She swiped panes on the tablet.

"Anonymous poetry. The end section. Between 'patisserie' and 'boulangerie.'"

I texted Thorn, who had wandered off, enchanted by

the mustiness, magic and decrepitude. She beat me to the place between "patisserie" and "boulangerie." She held the book in her hands. I crackled with an unexpected sense of resentment. I wanted to snatch it from her unworthy hands.

"Look," she said. The book fell open in her hands. Tucked between the pages, a letter. I read the heading: *Nanking, January 12th, 1937.*

"I have to have it."

The young woman at the Belle Epoque table looked up from her tablet.

'I can't sell that to you, sir.'

"But you have another one."

"Unfortunately, sir, the instructions . . ."

"Who can you sell it to?"

"Once again, sir . . ."

"The instructions . . ."

"We understand," Thorn said. "I'll put it back for you." Once we were out of sight of the woman at the Belle Epoque table Thorn snatched the book from my grasp. Once again I felt a spike of unwarranted jealousy. "You need to be a little bit more fen, Emmett," she said, took the letter, folded it, slipped it into her backpack and slid the book back into its place between "patisserie" and "boulangerie."

We nodded sincere thank-yous to the young woman

at the table and stepped through the courtyard's carriage door on Rue des Saints-Pères.

"Now buy me a fucking drink, Emmett Leigh."

I bought her a fucking drink, then another, then another, and we drank our way back across Paris to the Gare du Nord, and in the Gare du Nord and on the Eurostar. Only as the train entered the tunnel, when we felt safe from any chance of our small crime being discovered, did we open the letter and flatten it on the table. Thorn pressed close against me. The darkness of the tunnel was absolute.

Nanking,
January 12th, 1937

Tom my love,

I don't know where this letter will find you—or even if.

I am safe. All Europeans are inside the International Zone. Outside, the killing continues unabated. I made it out just ahead of the defeat at Shanghai on the next to last gunboat. China is lost: Chiang Kai-shek has withdrawn with the remains of his army deep into the west to Chungking, his capital is fallen and the Imperial Army of Japan engages in a butch-

ery that exceeds my capacity for horror.

Herr Rabe is of the opinion that it is only a matter of time before the Japanese tire of our posturing, end our pretense of governorship of the city and dismember our enclave. Yet his moral authority and his personal courage still stand between the two hundred and fifty thousand citizens of Nanking who have taken refuge inside the Safety Zone and the Imperial Army. He is unafraid to play the political card: at the worst of the bombing Rabe sent a cable to Berlin and within the week the Japanese had switched from indiscriminate air raids to attacking military and industrial targets. But we are never allowed to forget that we endure by sufferance. The soldiers outside our house pointedly unload and reload their weapons, or sharpen their bayonets.

Rabe fascinates me: a German, a Nazi, a party member with the ear of the Führer. He is a good man in hell. Yet I find it impossible not to regard him with the eye of what we have seen, what history has yet to see and judge him in the light of what his party and nation will unleash on humanity. It is also impossible not to wish, with that same foresight, that I had read more reports of this overlooked atrocity in what is to us a far and alien land. Rabe's concern for the people of the city, his revulsion at the atrocities carried on with unstinting enthusiasm beyond the safety of our small enclave, are genuine and heartfelt.

Am I a monster because, in the midst of a horror beyond even Christian imaginings of hell, I am relieved? Relieved because I had feared myself insensitive to horror. After everything we have seen, everything we have shared—and which pulls us back, time and time again—I find that there are horrors beyond even those of Gallipoli, Bosnia, the White War—here are horrors that spark emotion in me, revulsion, dread. A horror beyond even those of war, because it is both calculating and casual.

Butchery. Savagery. Atrocity. Again and again, these words. They do not suffice, yet there are no others. Outside our enclave, the Imperial Army unleashes violence beyond belief upon the citizens of Nanking. A third of the city lies in ruins. The mass executions continue daily: the sound of a firing squad is particular and distinctive, yet even the shootings are not enough. Magee tells me that he has photographed decapitation competitions; the soldiers see a Western photographer and push him to the front to show off their prowess. I have heard of mass drownings, burnings, live burials. I could write for pages of the sheer brutality of numbers—the beheading races, the bulldozings in mass graves—but it is the individual violations that offend most egregiously, because they are personal; calculatedly callous. The decapitated head with the cigarette placed in its mouth. The Chinese boy beaten to death with rifle butts because he refused to doff his hat to the soldiers. The man buried up to the neck and then stoned to death with bricks from his own home. The woman raped and shot, her skirt up over her face but her private parts exposed and propped open with a cane.

I walk between these abominations as if between burning pillars, immune but not immunized. Don't come to China, Ben. Wherever you are, stay there. I will find you. The world darkens and narrows; the places where we can communicate, where we can meet, are diminishing and departing. I believe Rabe when he says that the life of the Safety Zone is measured in days. What will happen I don't know. The civilians will be removed. What will happen to them I cannot say. The remaining Chinese soldiers will be exterminated. And the Europeans, the Americans? That's why the International Safety Zone Committee has decided someone must bear the testimony of the Rape of Nanking.

That's me.

McDaniel has given me a roll of undeveloped film, which I am smuggling downriver to Shanghai, where *it can be got to the Associated Press office and wired to the world. I am aboard a riverboat; HMS* Danae *is still running refugees from the Bund down to Hong Kong. I will only be a few days, a week at most, in Shanghai before the (as we now know) temporary safety of Hong Kong. Then I will try and get to Australia or South Africa.*

We drove through a hundred yards of bodies to reach the port. The dogs were already at work. Winter in Nanking is chilly, but the stench of rot—of mass, bloody death—followed us down the Yangtze for many miles. The Japanese searched me, of course. They confiscated my notebook, but left me the Time Was. *I will bring this one with me as far as I can, but I will leave messages in Shanghai and Hong Kong. The film of course they did not find.*

I know that I shall never be clean again. Some talk of scars, some talk of wounds, some of hurt and healing, but what I have seen here I can best describe as a pollution; a filth; a defilement not just of the body but of the soul; a deep stain, dyed into every fibre of me, that will never come out. Tattooed into my heart. And my great fear is that I won't find you, that this time we will each be whirled onward, never knowing. I couldn't bear to lose you. Even a moment, even our eyes meeting across the steps of the Madeleine, through the gloom of a London fog, would be enough.

Time was, time will be again,
Ben

The train came out of the tunnel into a different darkness. Our faces were reflected in the night-mirrored window. The passenger opposite us had fallen into a doze.

"Not immortals," Thorn said.

"No," I said. "Time travelers."

Shingle Street

A moment of beauty, now we are back in our separate worlds, separate corners of the pub. Ben and his Uncertainty Squad in Boffins Corner, me out on my window bench, writing, watching another autumn arrive hot and high. Thinking about him.

The bombers have shifted, the radar girls tell me; to night raids and the great cities of the North. Manchester has been badly blitzed. Ben is the scientist in a line of haberdashers and textile wholesalers: Seligman's warehouse in Salford was reduced to ashes. His family is unharmed. This in a few clipped exchanges at the bar as we buy fresh pints.

And Lizzie raises her eyebrows and swivels her eyes towards Boffins Corner when she comes out of the snug to order a new tray or drinks, and I smile, and dip my head, and she beams.

The Bawdsey Players are casting for a Murder Mystery. I've gone for a role, but if one is offered I shall decline. Ben Seligman will not be running the lights. The Uncertainty Squad works every hour on their experiment.

There's to be a demonstration, on a grain of salt. Men are up from London, men from the Ministry. If it goes well they'll move to a full field test.

"Explain it to me again."

We dawdle back to Bawdsey, a straggle of beery souls strung out along for half a mile along the street. We share cigarettes. This was the celebratory pint: tomorrow the Ministry men come to watch a grain of salt vanish.

"We place an object in a state of quantum superposition," Ben says. "The Heisenberg uncertainty principle sets a fundamental limit on what we may observe about physical systems. The more precisely an object's momentum is known, the less accurately we can measure its position. Its location becomes statistically uncertain—to all intents and purposes unobservable."

Ben has explained to me many times the principles of his work. His life is dedicated to the infinitesimal, the fragments of time, distance, matter. At the smallest levels, the universe operates according to very different rules from those of the sensual world. There are contradictions and impossibilities, paradoxes and strangenesses, a Lewis Carroll logic; yet this is the most accurate description of how reality works. There is nothing for me to hold to—no concrete truths, no sensory evidence, no inner visualization by which I might construct a meaning—but he appreciates my intrigue. I shared my world; he shares his. What I understand is that he sees a beauty—a sublime, something awesome and terrifying—that I do not.

I don't have the soul of a scientist. But I feel his excitement, his anxiety, his pride, his love.

The Uncertainty Squad waits by the guard hut; I go a different way from here.

~

He comes bounding into the dispatch room, white coat flapping. His glee is evident as he casts around through the fug of cigarette smoke. His eyes light on me, sprawled on the tattered sofa.

"Um, yes, you. I need you to take a message." He beckons me out to the where the bikes are parked. He keeps talking until we are clear of the building. "Sensitive stuff. Highest priority. Have to deliver it personally. Room on the back?"

I strap on my helmet and pull down my goggles.

"Where to, sir?"

"Just ride," Ben whispers in my ear. And we are off, his arms around my waist, the tails of his lab coat streaming out behind him. The MPs barely raise the pole in time as I swing onto Ferry Road.

"You should have gone for the Murder Mystery!" I

shout back into the slipstream. "That was a first-rate piece of acting."

I pull up at a field gate in a twin-rutted lane, under hawthorns, far from eyes. Ben fidgets, paces, can't keep still.

"We did it!" he shouts, throwing his arms up in an artless, unknowing hallelujah. "We achieved uncertainty for three minutes twenty-seven seconds. Three minutes twenty-seven!"

"All the lights dimmed," I say. "I felt the ground shake."

Ben is too excited to hear any words of mine. Suddenly, with the thrill of abandon, he takes my face between his hands and pulls me to him. We kiss.

Fenland

Looking back, I can see it began with the Nanking letter. We had stolen more than a letter. We had stolen a secret no one else knew, that no one else could know, for no one would understand. Shared secrets become shared madnesses. Shared madnesses become slow cancers.

The evidence was clear, in the accounts, the letters, the book that seemed to tie everything together. The conclusion was insane. No other conclusion was possible. We had intercepted the secret communications of two time travelers. Immortals I could have accepted—I argued my terms of belief the night of the Old Year storm—but time travelers outraged all my theories. If such creatures were actual, then we lived in a world of unscience. Miracles might be true. God might exist.

Through the late winter I hibernated in research like a dormouse curled in its nest. When the weather was bad, and it was that year, often—five times Doverhirne Drain over-topped the height gauge—I would not venture out of the house for days, hardly even stirring from Leland's study. Now that the old man confined his world to a well-worn track between bedroom, kitchen and toilet, I had colonized the Teu study—low ceilinged, small windowed, smelly—with my own books, fitted a Wi-Fi extender and bought a small electric oil heater from Spalding Poundland to supplement the ineffectual heating. Thorn brought me tea and bacon sandwiches when she remembered and I would usually remember to switch off the heater before sliding into bed beside her and nuzzling up to her round, solid warmth.

One week of stormy rain, I wandered among the stacks of great bookshops: La Sauterelle, Paris. Bertrand in Lisbon: the world's oldest, founded in 1732. Argosy in New York. Candide in Brussels. Vivalibri in Rome. All stocked copies of *Time Was*. Some held multiple copies. There had been more shops, I was certain—I had stumbled into the dying moments of The Golden Page and by accident intercepted a subtle network of dead drops and interleaved messages. Bookstores—book collectors, bookdealers—are stable, conservative, rooted creatures. Fashions and trends break around them; neighborhoods change, populations ebb and flow, but the bookshops and the books they hold close, these endure.

Until this post-literate age.

Time Was. A singular book. Eighty-eight pages. A list of contents: sixty-five numbered poems. No author biography, no foreword, no afterword, no index or notes. No publisher's address, no publication date. No print information, no edition number. It had never been filed with any of the receiving libraries. No other works by the author, no clue as to who the author might be. No reviews, no scholarly works, no exegesis, no references in any academic papers. A book that existed solely in the inventories of five bookshops.

It was the kind of private, esoteric code I might have devised myself.

For a short time I thought about asking my bibliophile friends to help me search for the book. There is Internet knowledge and there is private knowledge. I thought again. I didn't want them opening up my casket of secrets and peering inside. I loathed the idea of them taking my information and finding my time travelers. My time travelers.

Late snow came to the fen country, driving down hard across the North Sea, piling up along the hedge lines and turning the drains to ice. Leland stood for hours on end looking out of the kitchen window at the grey blizzarding across the back field. Thorn recalled stories her gram had told of winters when the rivers would freeze foot thick every year and Fenlanders held speed-skating contests. Leland was a four-times champion. He had been a strong, great-winded man then. One night the police in Pinchbeck picked Leland up from outside Tiffin's Cafe three minutes from hypothermia. He had walked the two miles from Hirne House to Pinchbeck in dressing gown and slippers. It took a week in drafty, inconsistently heated Hirne House to bring him back to warmth.

While Leland recovered and Thorn managed work on the house—Elder Würm had time off from gigging to get back to construction—I wrapped myself in a duvet and speculation. The careful, secret network of bookshops and literary dead drops left over decades seemed to indicate that my time travelers could not go home again. It also seemed to indicate that when they moved across time they did not always do so together. The mechanism would drop them in the same time period, give or take a few months—years—but often continents apart. That in turn suggested that their time traveling was not under their full control. Might, in fact, be involuntary. Lost in time.

I became an armchair time traveler. What I understood from my books and online chat was that the laws of physics held no theoretical bar to time travel, but in practice it required Big Stuff: the event horizons of black holes, space-time wormholes or piles of exotic matter somewhere in the region of the mass of Jupiter. Then there was the question of where—or rather when—Seligman and Chappell came from. Were they researchers from the future? Were they refugees? Were they visiting and returning, time and again? Were they time lost, unable to go home? Had there been an accident at the Department of Time Travel?

The thaw came suddenly; twelve degrees in one night, and by morning Doverhirne Drain was running an inch beneath our front door. The brown water receded leaving a pristine film of ocher mud through which the tips of the crocuses rose in small green nibs, and I realized spring was here and I had lost an entire season. I was pale and weak and cursed with a never-ending low-grade cold thanks to my depressed immune system. Thorn tried to get me out, get me into the light, get me with people, but I had nothing to talk about to her bike and rock friends Friday nights at the pub and I resigned from the Tuesday quiz nights before I was barred for being a fucking London smartarse. I walked during the day when no one else was around, and when Thorn was shuttling rehomed animals around the county in the Volvo I visited the pool in Spalding for laps and Jacuzzi, but my thoughts were lost in time, with Seligman and Chappell.

Site by site, Facebook group by Facebook group, history by history I filled in the gaps in my timeline. Chappell and Seligman were stitched through nineteenth- and twentieth-century history. Through the St. Petersburg Museum of Artillery I found a trace of them in the Russian Civil War of 1919, trapped in a winter-struck dacha with the remnants of the White Army retreating in disarray from St. Petersburg. From the Imperial War Museum in the North I found a possible sighting of Tom Chappell in the Crimea, bundled up for the Ukraine winter. Beards and furs made identification tentative. The photograph was dated 1856. I found them on the bridge of HMS *Jamaica* at Inchon; I came across them again at a table outside a hotel in Saigon.

Quantum theory holds that the physical reality of the electron is a wave function, a range of probabilities of the particle's energy and position. There are locations where the probability of the electron existing is small but still non-zero; there are locations where the probability is almost 100 percent. The probabilities follow the bell-shaped normal distribution curve. Chappell and Seligman's trajectory through time followed a similar distribution, I surmised. You can tell how far I had wandered from world and humanity that I was spinning quasi-mystical quantum-magical theories out of my head. I plotted my data; I drew up probabilities. If 1856 and Crimea were the lower lower third sigma, then I could find the upper limit on my timeline.

Riddled with holes, weak data, assumptions and wishful thinking, I did the sums.

The upper three-sigma limit was approximately 2,030.

Obsession is a soft, creeping dementia. As with the loss of the mind, you always believe that everything is well, everything is good and right, everything is normal. Wonderful. At the start. It was only reasonable that I could move back to the Frig room—I was keeping strange, troubling hours and Thorn had work. Never a stout Fens yeoman, I was losing weight I could not afford: I skipped meals, grazed from the fridge, lived for days on weak milky tea. Thorn stopped me from eating a three-day-moldy loaf I found in the back of the bread bin. When I caught what I thought was a spring flu in that damp, drafty room, I still insisted on working through it, even when it steepened sharply into pneumonia and I was taken to Peterborough City Hospital with a tap in my chest. My temperature peaked at 39.5 degrees, I hallucinated I was shattered into a thousand mirror shards of myself and had to search through my parallel faces to find the one that wore a star-shaped bindi of cosmic consciousness called the Sai-wism. I returned to Hirne House to find spring unfolding into early summer. Thorn's metal friends were making good time on the extension; I sat in a folding chair in the sun looking across the scraggy lawn to Leland in his chair and felt as old and insane as he. I blinked in the sun and thought myself well. I had been a long way, to a strange place, and I had returned. When I first noticed, then commented, then shouted that the construction noise was stopping my concentrating on my work—my work! I had travelers to hunt down through the crannies of time!—I realized that what had returned to Hirne House was not what had departed.

One day the sun was neither so high nor so long that I could sit in it anymore. Leaves blew into the corners of the garden. I checked the date. I had been over a year on the fen country, this flat, open land where nothing could hide yet which seemed more full of secrets than any place in London.

The shift indoors prodded my mind out of its rut. I returned to the Emmett Leigh theory of time travel. The lowest points of probability on my carefully constructed distribution curve were 1840 and 2030. The thing I had not realized, the thing I could not see until it came out of the sun, like a blinding solar god revealing himself to me, was the peak of maximum probability. My records and researches showed the highest incidence of traces of Chappell and Seligman between 1935 and 1949.

They were not time travelers from the future. They were time travelers from the past.

~

To celebrate the completion of the new extension—

headachy with fresh gloss paint, carpet so fresh you could sign your name in the pile—Thorn had desecrated its pristine plaster with a new seventy-two-inch 4K television. Full surround sound. She had bought it from a mate down the pub. Rural economics.

I insisted we christen it by watching the documentary again.

'"All of it?" Thorn asked.

"Just the bit," I conceded.

The 4K did little for the low-def picture, but the sound was magnificent. For the first time I could make out Chappell's words clearly. I could discern that he had an accent.

"He's an East Anglia boy," Thorn said.

I had been long enough in the flat country to understand that a slew of dialects was voiced from Boston to Chelmsford to Cambridge, but I would never be local enough to identify the micro-accents.

"Leland would know," Thorn said. "Talk six words to him and he can pinpoint the parish."

It took the better part of the morning to get Leland in a seat, with the DVD, watching, listening and comprehending my questions.

"What? Who is that person? I don't know him."

"For the love of fuck," I exploded for the twentieth time.

"He's an old man, Emmett," Thorn said with frost in her voice. "You're scaring him."

I played the DVD again.

"East Suffolk," Leland declared with a sudden strength and sonority that made me appreciate how he could have led a coven of his own private paganism. "Ipswich, Woodbridge. Play it again."

I did.

"Seaside. The Sandings."

It took me the better part of a week to summon up the courage to break my hermeticism, so soon after London, and arrange for a pint with Lee, Elder Würm's sometimes sound engineer, village esotericist and self-proclaimed Aelder Kin of Hilderwic. We sat in the snug over pints of terrible lager. He could not have been more uncomfortable had he been up in front of a judge.

"Good job on the extension," I said. "The paint's finally stopped giving me headaches."

"Cool," Lee said. "Um. Good. Good."

He still looked as if he wanted to run.

"There's something I want to ask you," I said.

He froze. His hand shook so badly he had to set his pint down to keep from spilling it.

"Are you all right?"

He nodded, terrified.

"You know about myths and weird shit," I said. "Down

Ipswich, Woodbridge way, are there any strange local legends? Recent?"

Relief spread over his face. He downed half his pint in one swallow."

"Are you fucking kidding? Rendlesham, hello?"

He had an afternoon: I had a lifetime. He took me.

∼

Woods have always disquieted me. I may have been over-exposed to fairy tales in my early years—I was a sickness-prone kid, my education came as much from the books I read as from school, but I have never lost the belief in the eyes that watch from between the roots. The trees rearrange themselves when your back is turned. Even in a new Forestry Commission plantation. If anything, the rows of regularly spaced, identical pulpwood conifers are more sinister.

Lee told me the story on the drive down. Rendlesham was the site of the UK's major UFO incident.

"Britain's Roswell, man," Lee said. It all seemed the standard mix of the inconsequential and the conspiratorial: US Air Force base, farm animals in a frenzy, lights in the wood, one uncorroborated witness. Rendlesham true believers had marked out a UFO trail. Despite the friendly signposts—marked with the standard oval-eyed grey alien—I became increasingly uncomfortable as we worked along the forest paths deeper into the wood, partly from my innate sense of the uncanny, partly from the growing evidence of the things people do when they are far from the gaze of others. Mountain bikers had created a complete network of tracks, jumps, log bounces, berms, plank walks despite the terrain being flat as a sheet of paper. We came across scorched remnants of campfires, beer cans, WKD bottles, condoms. Needles. Totems woven from twigs. A burned-out car.

"Did you ever do a ritual down here?" I asked Lee. "In your Aelder of Hilderwic capacity?"

"In Rendlesham? You fucking kidding, man?"

Lights in the night. Isolated, suggestible people. I understood the power of the wild wood. If I had not been looking for something other—time travel, not space—I could have believed. I wanted to believe. I did not, until we came to the high point of the expedition, the clearing where the object had touched our Earth. The enthusiasts who had set the trail had marked the point with three wooden poles. Lee had saved the photographs to his phone and showed me the original markings. I stood in the center of the triangle of posts. I felt . . . something.

Not quite a whisper, not quite the wind. Not quite lights in the sky, not quite the lowering autumn sun. Not quite space, not quite time. I felt uncertain. I felt loosely tethered to the world. Everything seemed very close yet infinitely distant at the same time. I saw figures among the trees; I saw mountain bikers slipping past on their secret paths. I thought I might throw up. I stepped out of the triangle. Sharp in my mind was an idea that hadn't been there before. Quantum events may occur spontaneously. And recur. Everything is a probability.

"You okay?"

I pleaded my long recuperation. This wasn't the place. But it was tied to the place, entangled.

"Are there any other weird stories about this area?" I asked as we trudged back to the van.

"Can't move for them," Lee said.

"Say around the time of the Second World War?"

"Are you shitting me?" I wished Lee could answer just one of my questions without casting doubt on my wit or sanity. "We're less than five miles from Shingle Street."

I also hated his habit of half-answering my questions by inviting another.

"Shingle Street?"

"The sea caught fire. Charred bodies on the beach. Some weird shit went down on that Suffolk coast. They'll tell you it never happened, it's all rumors and urban legends. That's the first level of cover-up. They're clever, see? Then there's the second level: it was really a botched German invasion and they set the sea on fire. Most people go away satisfied with that. They lift the mask and see what's underneath, but what's underneath, Emmett, is another mask. The truth is under that mask. The truth is out there, like the show says."

"How would I see that truth?"

"What do you want it see for, friend?"

Lee's commitment to paranoia was as legendary as his consumption of hydroponic skunk. I told him the truth. I was looking for time travelers. These things worked both ways. He could tell who he liked and no one would believe him. We were at the van now and Lee fished a Tesco receipt out of a car pocket and wrote a name and a number on the back.

"He's the man. Shingle Street, born, bred and buttered. Wise in the ways. You know?"

On the drive back to Hirne House I researched Shingle Street on my phone. The place was right: the Sandings, the pebble coast between Felixstowe and Aldeburgh. The time was right: the legends around Shingle Street dated from 1940.

I had found my time travelers' point of departure.

~

A sudden construction job came up for Lee, so Thorn drove me down to Shingle Street. She brought the dogs.

They would enjoy the beach. It was a two-hour drive and they became fractious within ten minutes of home.

I had researched the location through images and maps, street view and Pinterest, through oral history and fake history and official history, conspiracy theory and fiction, through ghosts and legend, but the reality still surprised me. Words and pictures cannot carry the crunch of sea-rounded stone under the tires as we pulled into the car park, the salt-sweet perfume of the grasses, the scabbing dryness of the air, the knock of a hundred million pebbles rolling in the wave lap. I felt exposed and agoraphobic under a sky more huge than that of Lincolnshire, watched by unseen eyes. To the south, beams of sunlight struck through breaks in the cloud layer: God's searchlights. The row of houses, the seaside cottages, the old Martello tower down the beach were the only verticals, yet they seemed to cower in this land of overwhelming horizontals. I could not imagine how anyone lived with any degree of sanity in such an unrelenting landscape. The dogs did not burst from the back of the car in their customary excitement. They clung close, weaving around our legs as we walked up the beach towards the Martello where we would meet Regenbald Howe. Thorn threw a stick into the sea to try to lift the dogs' disquiet. Cwen, most aquatic of mutts, fretted up and down the shingle, whining, dancing back from the lap of water.

I had never been to such an uncanny place.

Regenbald Howe was a man of slate and wire, hollow faced, skin turned to leather, long grey hair tied in a silver ring. He was a Jarl of Hilderwic; he wore a pierced pebble on a thong around his neck, inscribed with the Ash rune. He wore technical outdoors gear from Decathlon and carried a long, twisted walking stick that he informed us was a dried bull's pizzle, a powerful ritual object.

He marched us past the houses and the charred ribs of the Lifeboat Inn to the old Martello tower. I have always been fascinated by Martello towers, that chain of lookouts built along the coast of Britain and Ireland at the height of Napoleonic paranoia, but I had never been inside one.

"I just keep an eye on the place," Regenbald told us as the tip of his bull pizzle clicked up the metal staircase to the door halfway up the leeward curve of the tower. "Let in the renters."

The decor was London rural weekend: resculpted brick, furniture designed to fit the curving walls; spiral staircases and the glass cupola at the top where we sat on semi-circular benches, watched November spread like a bruise along the eastern horizon and hoped for the offer of something warming. The pizzle stick was propped against the wall by the light switch. The dogs slumbered on their sides in the kitchen, legs reaching straight out.

"So, what nonsense have they told you?" Regenbald asked. I told him the wartime legends: the sea set ablaze; the rumors of a botched German invasion, the bodies of dead Nazis strewn along half a mile of beach, hideously burned; the mysterious lights and sounds that traveled long across sea and shingle. The theory that the government had carried out an experiment so unholy that it had polluted even the stone, sea and spirit of Shingle Street, so ghastly that all knowledge of it had been rigorously suppressed and made incredible by a campaign of misinformation and rumormongering.

"And what do you believe?" Regenbald said.

Thorn and I shifted in our seats and exchanged secretive glances.

"That Shingle Street was the location of a secret government Second World War time-travel experiment," I said.

"Time travel?" Regenbald said with a haughtiness that made me feel like sliding down the spiral stairs and running as fast and far as I could from this judgmental place.

"We found . . . evidence," I said weakly.

"Chappell and Seligman," Howe said. His Suffolk accent was as slow and broad as the horizon. "They were stationed at RAF Bawdsey during the war. It was the center of the Home RADAR network, but there were a lot of War Ministry research projects going on. I know nothing about time travel, but I do know there was something called the Uncertainty. Ben Seligman was a boffin in the research division, a Northerner, a Manc. But Tom Chappell, he's proper Sandings. Local boy. There are still Chappells up in Bawdsey village. Used to run the ferry. You'll find Tom Chappell in the parish records: baptized St. Mary's June 12, 1914. He's still up on the sports team boards at Felixstowe Grammar: cross-country running. Set the county under-sixteen record. Bit of a local poet."

I was vertiginous with wonder. That is the only word in our language, but it cannot convey the emotion of those tectonic truths closing with a sound like trumpets, the physical sense of being at the same time huge and small, a feeling like acceleration of the universe receding and at the same time racing in towards me.

"You're ready to read the diary now," Howe said. He took a fabric-wrapped package from inside his weather-proof jacket, laid it on the conversation table and unfolded a great length of soft muslin. The diary was a soft tan wad the size of a cigarette packet. It was all I could do to keep myself from snatching it up and opening it. "The family didn't get it back until 1980. None of the material to do with Bawdsey Manor was ever declassified, but someone left it on their doorstep."

"Same year as the Rendlesham event," I said.

Howe took a long pause before continuing.

"The family didn't know what to do with it—the Chappells in Bawdsey were quite old by then; most of the younger generations had moved away—so they gave it to me, as the last Jarl, and keeper of the coast." He handed the diary to me; I took it like a sacrament. "I've marked some passages that might be of interest to you."

Thorn huddled up beside me to read with me, but the book was tiny, the pencil handwriting minuscule and the light in the glass cupola fading. I threw on every lighting source in the round room and read aloud.

Shingle Street

Ben calls on the field telephone from the Martello tower.

"Get yourself up here, Tom."

The boldness. On an open line. But this place has made us bold: open and exposed.

"Back of the tower."

All the bikes are on standby to run messages back to Bawdsey in case of an unexpected breakdown in communications. The Uncertainty Squad thinks it a distinct possibility. The electrical and magnetic energies they will generate are powerful enough to disrupt radio communications, even telephone lines. I steal a pushbike from the back of the other-ranks mess, sneak it over the fence, and I'm off up Buckanay Lane. Not that anyone would care. There's been a madness over Bawdsey all week, a crazed holiday spirit, a last-day-of-term wildness. Everyone has been up to see the barge moored off Shingle Street.

Tonight, for one night only: Before your very eyes! Abracadabra!

No one quite knows what to expect, not even Ben and his Uncertainties. The Ministry men saw him make a flake of sea salt disappear. This is a sea barge. Will the barge disappear from sight? Will it suddenly be surrounded by a hundred phantom barges? Will its double appear in the sea three weeks—or even three years from now? All of those? Bawdsey has dispatched observers up and down the coast for twenty miles.

The most likely, and most dull, result is that nothing will happen.

Ben is with the group in the Shingle Street Martello tower.

I see him light a cigarette in the tower door. I answer with a match flare; he nods and lifts his binoculars, camera, tin hat and clipboard. I hear him shout about checking the forward observation position. I follow him to one of the abandoned fishermen's houses.

"This is insane," I say.

"It's always been insane," Tom says. "Come on. Quick."

I have known these houses and felt their disapproval for peering through the salt-streaked windows. To enter one is a violation. All the things I glimpsed are actual. I can smell the blue mold from the ancient loaf. I feel the chill from that damp, leaking corner of the kitchen ceiling. There is a coal scuttle and old newspaper, frozen in time, under the stairs.

Tom sets up the observation post in the kitchen.

"I wish you'd brought that Primus," he says. "I could

murder a cup of tea."

I borrow Ben's binoculars. The Uncertainty betrays little of its complex theory. The barge is moored a hundred yards offshore. Wires and antennae festoon the mast; I can easily make out boxy shapes under tarpaulins in the hold.

I shiver with excitement, not just from my thrilling elopement with Ben, but because I am about to witness the fruit of his work. He has explained to me time and again the theory and the engineering, but it is a secret world to me.

"Is that generator on the boat?"

"Auxiliary power," Ben explains. "We're running the main power down a cable from shore."

A boat of age-greyed wood on a grey sea as flat as sheet iron, grey sky, grey stone, grey November. Two men freezing in an abandoned kitchen, watching for it to disappear.

I start to giggle at the silliness. Ben catches my gaiety and together we roar with helpless laughter, doubled up over the kitchen table.

Ben glances at his watch and hilarity flees.

"Two minutes. We should be counting down to initial power-up."

"Have you any idea how sexy you sound?" I say, and move towards him.

Ben steps away. "Work to do, darling."

Then the room, the house, every pebble of Shingle Street throbs. A mighty chord, deeper than any bass, shakes me to the marrow in my backbone.

"Initial power-up?" I say.

"That's only twenty percent," Ben says, and the house, the floor beneath my feet, the air itself throbs again to a new power spike.

"It feels like this place is going to come in around us," I say.

We grab binoculars, clipboard, the accoutrements of Uncertainty, and flee. Outside, the dour November air is alive with energy. Sky, stone, sea beat with a vast primal song.

"Is it meant to be like this?" I shout.

"I don't know!" Ben shouts back. "Isn't it extraordinary?"

Even without the binoculars I can see something is happening to the barge. Balls of Saint Elmo's fire roll up and down the masts, the sheets, the cables. The sea around it seems as transparent as glass, seems to glow from beneath. Mirage barges flicker in and out of existence; for whole moments windows seem to open in the sky, through which I glimpse what I can only describe as other seas, other skies.

Ben cranks up the radio.

"This is Coastguard cottage forward position," he yells. "We are experiencing unusual atmospheric and electrical phenomena. Over."

The radio crackles once in reply, then Ben cries out and drops the handset.

"I don't think I'm going to be reporting back to the Martello," Ben says. I hug him, pull him to me. The pulse of power almost knocks me to the ground. Every pebble seems to lift and separate from every other; every spear of sea grass blazes. Every object is haloed in the light. The glow from the sea is blinding.

"Eighty percent!" Ben shouts. "Magnificent!"

T minus twenty seconds, on my old wristwatch, though I can't trust it, can't trust anything.

"Full power," Ben announces, and my bones thrum with power and I can see into everything, every cell and particle. I catch a flicker of motion in the house behind us. I look around. I see us, in the kitchen. And on the path from the Martello tower, and at the door to the Martello tower: us.

"Uncertainty," Ben says.

~

We kiss and the sea catches fire.

Fenland

"They were lovers," I said. "Time-crossed lovers. All the best stories are love stories."

Thorn drove with savage concentration. By the time we left Shingle Street it was thick dark, we were down to one headlight and a warm front was moving in, with buffets of wind and rain that challenged the one working windscreen.

"All the stories say the sea caught fire. Flames leaping a thousand feet into the sky. But that's just another way of describing what Amal saw at Gallipoli: the Lost Battalion marching up into the glowing cloud. It's the same thing: a thing no one had seen before, that had never existed until they threw the switch up in the tower. There are no words to describe what they saw. They thought they were building a cloaking device; instead, they created a time storm—no, a time *vortex*."

"Doctor Who, Emmett. Fuckin' Doctor Who."

"I felt it, Thorn, at Rendlesham. It's the same thing: it wasn't some alien spacecraft; it was the time vortex, touching Earth again."

After Ben Chappell's diary, Regenbald showed me the witness statements, personal records, annotations in family Bibles, letters, urban legends jotted down in draughty church halls, World War 2 re-enactor meets, greasy-spoon cafes, living rooms smelling of damp dog, over-heated pub inglenooks: the stories of the Time the Sea Caught Fire. The barge had disappeared; the barge had been seen at Harwich, Aldeburgh, Southwold, Great Yarmouth, as far afield as Cromer and Southend—all at the same time, the barge was waiting stogged in the sand when the Fiftieth Infantry went ashore at Gold Beach on D day. The observers were all sworn to secrecy. The observers all went mad. The observers all died. Burning bodies washed up on the tide. On days of strange calm and overcast, when sea and sky and shingle seemed to merge, burning figures could be seen standing on the water, just beyond the break line. On days of strange calm and overcast, on those days when the elements merged with one another, a cloud could sometimes be seen moving in from the sea, low and dark and always driving against the wind, a cloud flickering with lightning and the mutter of thunder, though some witnesses claimed to have heard voices, or a terrible animal roaring from it.

They wanted to make a ship invisible. They wanted to make a ship insubstantial as a ghost. They wanted to open a portal to another universe. They wanted to open a gate to hell.

"They tried to make it uncertain in space and time," Regenbald said. "They succeeded, but not with the ship."

"One thing I still don't get," I ranted. "The book. *Time Was*. Tom must have had it with him, but I still don't understand where it came from."

"Emmett . . ."

"E.L. must have been some mentor figure, but who was he?"

"Emmett, I need to tell you something."

"He turns up, gives Tom a book of his own poems, does the full Yoda, then disappears."

"Emmett, I really—"

"Thorn, Thorn, maybe there are more than two time travelers!"

"It'll do tomorrow, Emmett."

～

There was no point at which I could be certain that that I lived with Thorn. There certainly was a point when I unlived with her.

The morning after we came back from Shingle Street she told me, over tea and *Homes Under the Hammer* on the big screen in the new extension, what had been so urgent in the car. She had been fucking Lee for six months. Lee and every member of Elder Würm except Phil the drummer, who was into stuff she didn't like.

That was how the build had gone so quickly.

~

The English bloom in Rome.

The shop closed late, but I stayed later, chasing the readers, the sitters, the chatters and the trysters, the old men aching to take the weight off their feet and the ones so deep in their books they had lost all notion of time. Before I locked up I checked the E.L.s. I had safeguards in place: I was to be informed if anyone inquired about him. He sat in his careful place, in the middle of the third row from the top in a narrow rack of shelves at the end of a stack. I could keep an eye on him from both the till and the performance space, the parts of the shop where I was most occupied.

My apartment was as small and full of books as my vile rooms in Clapham but the voices of a different city entered it and engaged my senses: children protesting, television, arguments, electronic dance music and instrument practice. Doubtless the same banalities, misapprehensions and rages I heard in London, but in Italy, in *Rome,* they were the lexicon of life. I ate hastily: spaghetti with oil, garlic and chilli with a glass of wine. Then I would step out. On Mondays, Wednesdays, Fridays and Sundays I went to the

Campogiani. The other days I would visit L'Oasi della Birra. I took my customary tables—both with views of the shop—and drank wine commensurate with my Wi-Fi use.

I stayed until one, one thirty, then slept until the light through my sagging blinds woke me. Espresso at Linari. Three sips watching the shop, always an eye on the shop.

Every day for two and a half years now.

I had doubted Rome. I saw myself as a Paris type, a haunter of cafes and bookstores, a latter-day flaneur. La Sauterelle closed, followed by Candide in Brussels. The age of the general bookstore, when serendipities lay in corners that smelled of cat piss and the dust bags of vacuum cleaners, was closing. Grubby little dealers like me with my eBay store and my business run out of Thorn's barn were the small assassins.

We'd come to an agreement over the business, amicably worked out on social media, but I didn't friend her and didn't go to the funeral when Gram Leland died that December: a wander too far, too late, barefoot on a frozen road, drowning by hypothermia in Doverhirne Drain.

I doubted Rome, but both Paris's and Brussels's copies of *Time Was* went to the dead drops in Testaccio. It seemed like a sign. I went in the early autumn, when Rome is unspeakably lovely. Autumn sun charmed me, seduced me, woke me; low sun, the kindest sun. I went to

Vivalibri, went straight to the *Time Was*, lifted it, took it to the till. I could feel no additions or insertions. I told a fearful, wonderful lie.

"I know you are not allowed to sell it to me," I said. "*Le Istruzioni*. I am an agent of the Instructions, and I have been instructed to watch over the books and ensure that they get to their intended recipient."

Signor Manzoni's eyes bulged; then his face broke into a monstrous grin at my sheer chutzpah. I started the next day. The pay was lousy. Whoever said it is easier to be poor in a warm climate never lived in Testaccio in the middle of gentrification. Had I arrived five years before I could have lived cheaply, in the manner befitting a British bibliophile. The non-Catholic cemetery off the Via Caio Cestio was full of low-rent English, from Keats to Richard Mason. Now rents were spiraling, and I faced the additional nonsense of post-Brexit residency paperwork.

My first night, after I chased the readers, sitters, chatters, trysters, sore old men and the book lost, I went online to do the thing I had neglected all the years I had been chasing Chappell and Seligman across the centuries, the obvious thing I had overlooked in my intrigue at the world the Alexandria letter had opened up: the what happened next?

It was easy to find.

~

A glass of wine at the window, an eye on the bookstore, Wi-Fi and the papers. There was a ritual to this too. You start with the online quality dailies—*la Repubblica, Corriere della Sera, La Stampa,* your lips moving as your Italian strains at the copy. You read the headlines, the front pages, the international news. You search out the matter of Britain, does England stand? With time you turn first to the sport—never less than entertaining in Rome—then you add the celebrity gossip. Time again, you drift away from the big papers to the evening press, the local news. Buried treasure lies here. The school graduations, the masses and novenas, the pilgrimages. The stoic reporting of dreadful micro-league football; the court reports, made piquant by the possibility that you might have witnessed or overheard the incident. The joys and heartbreaks folded inside every classified advertisement; the deaths, marriages, births. Accounts of strange and unnatural occurrences from distant regions, like a freak storm in Cyprus; a ball of wind and lighting and dry thunder that clung to a valley side just outside Polystipos, defying wind and nature. It hung there for three days, said a priest. Every animal fled, said a local horse breeder. "My olives and fruit trees have been blighted," said the boardinghouse owner. "I heard voices coming out of it," a taxi driver said. "I saw the face of the devil in it," said the local eccentric.

The time storm had come, and with it a traveler.

I gave him time. He would have to find out where he was, when he was, learn that there were only three dead drops left in the world where he might find a message, or leave a message, and make his way around them. In time he would come down into Testaccio and make his way across the piazza to Vivalibri.

Summer flowed into autumn.

I was having lunch at Linari when my phone played Thomas Dolby. Since I learned there was a piece of music called "Cloudburst at Shingle Street" nothing else could be my alert that a traveler had stepped out of time into my bookshop.

Tazia had given him one of the leather club chairs in the performance space, and a coffee. I studied him from the across the shop. An Englishman in his late thirties, experience lines beginning to set around his eyes and mouth. Tanned. About my age, I realized. Not so much older than my last image of him, in his private, patchwork chronology, smiling at the pyramids, his arm around the shoulder of his lover.

I died inside.

He looked as if he wanted to run, if there were anywhere he could run.

I had been rehearsing my words for three years.

"Tom Chappell," I said.

He looked up. I saw astonishment, terror, wonder, but most of all *recognition,* on his face. He knew me.

My prepared speech evaporated.

"Emmett?" he said, eyes wide with awe. "Emmett Leigh?"

~

The shop unfolded around me. The books sprang from their shelves and took flight on broken-spined wings. The shelves tumbled like Rome itself falling. I found myself sitting on the floor in a wheel of impossibilities.

I may have stammered, "W-w-what?"

"Time was," Chappell said.

People were staring at me: the readers, the sitters, the chatters and trysters, the aching old men and the book lovers.

I had said to Thorn, *Maybe there are more than two time travelers*!

Emmett Leigh. E.L.

Tazia had sat me up and was glaring at Chappell.

"Is this man bothering you?" she asked me.

"No," I said weakly, waving my hands at the reality beyond the rows of books, the polite, peering faces.

"I saw him fall down," said one of the old men.

Now Signor Manzoni had a hand on my arm.

"Did you push him?" he demanded of Chappell.

"You don't understand," I raved. "There were more than two time travelers. The man with the book, it was me. All along."

"The signor is unwell," Signor Manzoni said as he and Tazia helped me to the staff room. Chappell followed me. Tazia firmly barred entry.

"We have to talk," Chappell said.

"Sir, I think it would be better if you left," Tazia said. Her English was better. The world reeled around me, punch-drunk as Signor Manzoni seated me. I saw Chappell write a hasty note and give it to Tazia before she closed the door on him.

A time and a garden.

~

On the Aventine Hill are two gardens. The Giardino degli Aranci is gracious and spacious, shaded by umbrella pines and orange trees. Tourists flock to this garden to take selfies on the parapet with its heartbreaking views along the Tiber to St. Peter's. The Giardino di Sant'Alessio is smaller, quieter, more restrained, tucked in beside the Basilica of Saints Boniface and Alexius. Its views are constrained, its prospect less spectacular, its shade less generous, but it is quiet and gracious with space and time. I spent much time here, immuring myself with the present against a past I now understood as mediocre, vacillating, insignificant. If I died today, no one would know I was gone from the world.

We sat on a stone bench. An elderly lady, rocking with arthritis, ambled with a tiny dog. A young woman in sportswear performed a sun salutation at the parapet. Two men in hi-vis sat on the matching bench across the main path and frowned at their phones.

"You told me about this place," Chappell said. "The gardens of the Aventine: there's the one the tourists go to . . ."

"And the one the Romans go to," I said.

"Shingle Street, 1937," Chappell said. "November. Filthy weather. Five days before you disappeared. I never saw you again."

He left the *until* . . . unspoken.

"My uncle was diagnosed with terminal cancer at the age of forty-seven," I said. "He smoked and he smoked and he smoked and cancer came and killed him quickly."

"I'm sorry," Chappell said.

"I always wondered how he felt when the doctor told

him he had weeks to live. I think I know now."

In the Giardino di Sant'Alessio the two workmen got up from their bench and shambled past, plaster-spattered boots crunching the pink gravel, nodding greetings.

I was the mentor figure who had given him the book of poems, poems that had always seemed to the seventeen-year-old Tom to speak to him personally, to address his particular hopes and fears and confusions. I was the figure who had been waiting by the Martello tower as he made his lonely, searching walks up the street of stones. The figure who first exchanged nods, then greetings and observations on the weather, observations that became deeper musings on the state of the world. That became conversations that explored the boy's hopes, mysteries, dreads and dreamings, the things that made him different from the other boys in his village

"'Storm's coming,' you always said. Even on the clearest days," Tom said. "I didn't understand."

"I could have told you," I said. I gave a small, sour smile. "It's a linguistic offense, finding a grammar for talking about a thing long since said that have I have yet to say."

"You couldn't, though, could you?" Tom said, and I understood the paradoxes of time through which he had lived. Time protects itself. To have warned Tom would have unmade whatever lay ahead of me that would send me through the doors of time.

Everything came back to the grey stone road of Shingle Street.

In my Testaccio exile I have refined my theories of time travel. My best theory for what Ben Seligman and the Uncertainty Squad attempted at Shingle Street was to manifest quantum effects in the classical universe, to apply Heisenberg's uncertainty principle to a macro-scale object by entangling all of its atoms into one quantum state. All the components of that single state remain connected, however far removed from one another in space and time. What affects a single part affects all others. What Seligman could not have known was they would be drawn into the entangled state. Might indeed have become the entangled state, by some misalignment of the apparatus. What I could not have known was that I too was entangled with them, through an event that lay before me, which I could not avoid, as immense and final as death.

The sun shone on us on our stone bench, time traveler and time traveler to be.

"Do you know how it happens?" I asked.

"It's complicated," Tom said. "There is the historical timeline and there are our timelines through it. I've only ever met you once. But we may meet—will meet—again and again further along our timelines. What I can say is that when I met you—meet you—on Shingle Street, you look the age you are now."

Soon then.

"I went to Rendlesham," I said. "There's some story about a UFO—"

"Nonsense," Tom said.

"I know. It was some afterglow from the original event. I felt it."

"It resonated through time and space, like harmonics in a plucked string. We are carried along the nodes."

The yoga woman ended her routine, rolled up her mat, rolled past us with an exhibitionist swagger.

"I'm scared," I said.

"When I came out of it that first time, not recognizing where I was, then realizing that I didn't even know when I was, I was terrified," Tom said. "You learn. There are tricks. You cache things across time. You become an expert in false identities. We're like spies. Those are the practicalities. The important thing, the true thing, is that I know I'm not alone."

'Tom."

He looked startled by my use of his first name, the shift of my tone from apprehension to tenderness.

"I have to give you something." Since I heard of the time storm opening, I had kept the Alexandria letter next to my heart. Now I handed it to Tom.

"I found it in the closing-down sale for The Golden Page."

He read it, folded it, held it in two hands.

"I wrote that only a few weeks ago, in my timeline. I flew to Malta, then came back to London by ship. I half-expected to find The Golden Page bombed to rubble. It was still there. Hawksmoor's Christ Church still stood. It's a strong place; time snags around it. It protects Spitalfields. I left the book and that letter. I waited. War is the great uncertainty. Then I felt the tug—you'll learn this—like electricity in the brain, like a hand around my heart, pulling me. So, the next one, I thought. He is dead, isn't he?"

"Yes. I'm sorry."

Tom sat still, straight, his hands flat on his thighs, looking ahead over Rome.

After a long silence he said, "It was always my great fear. Sometimes we would fail to find each other and there was always that terrible, chewing dread that the other had died. What happened?"

"The *Carmarthen Castle* was attacked and sunk by Italian torpedo bombers one hundred and thirty miles north of Algiers. There were two thousand five hundred men aboard. Five hundred and twelve survived."

Again, silence. I knew he saw nothing but that ship, sailing beyond the arms of the harbor, into grief beyond words, beyond expression.

"Can I have any hope?"

"There's a list of all the survivors."

"He's not on it."

"No. No one knew for years. Decades. The War Office embargoed the information for fear of its effect on morale."

"The British love of secrecy," Chappell hissed suddenly. "Stupid, stupid, stupid boy. Stupid way to die." He looked up at the shading canopy of the pines. "We adored this city. We came here in 1944 after the American liberation. You can't imagine the place. The streets were empty. We went to St. Peter's. The Pope was still addressing the faithful on Sundays. The Vatican was like a little bubble in time. All of Rome was, like a hole in the war. It was strange; it was magical. We came up here. How could I not? I wonder if sometimes Ben felt he was following in your shadow."

"I was following in his shadow."

"We will cross lives. I know it. I'll see him; on the Rialto in 1918, in the walls of the Kalemegdan in Belgrade in 1993. Saigon, 1969, across a bar. I won't say a word. I can't say a word. I can't even let him see me."

He took the letter from his jacket and unfolded it carefully.

"I can still see the lights of the Western Harbour. The

sound of guns carried such a long way, all the way from El Alamein. The lake does strange things to sound. The night was so still, I could hear the sound of boat engines long after it disappeared from my sight. So little time. So little time!"

Now the old woman was leading her dog up the gravel path to the gate. The garden was ours.

"Don't leave me," Chappell said, reaching out a hand on the warm stone of the bench. I rested my hand on his. I couldn't leave him. We were the lost men, the bereaved men, the loneliest men in the universe. We were entangled.

~

I saw figures among the trees at Rendlesham. I saw myself, shattered across time. Nodes, harmonics, resonances up and down the timeline. I had touched an echo, basked in the afterglow of the Shingle Street event when Ben Seligman and his Uncertainty Squad brought the quantum, probabilistic world into touch with our world of discrete space and distinct time. An insight came to me among the trees and mountain-bike runs: that quantum events may occur and recur spontaneously. Everything is possible.

I'm afraid. But I won't be alone.

~

I check my kit every morning. It all fits into one small leather bag—leather. Plastics, artificial fabrics, rub up against the grain of history. Classic shoes, also leather. A hat, timeless. Rainproofs. Sleeping bag, matches. I still must find a natural-fiber sleeping bag. Penicillin and other over-the-counter antibiotics. Tinned food, water-sterilizing tablets, a multitool. A sewing kit. A couple of gold coins, stitched into the lining of the bag. Two watches: one to tell the time, one to sell. Jewelry. Rings, blings, glittery things. Wearable wealth.

I hate the look of myself in jewels. I console myself that somewhere, out there, perhaps in this city, perhaps in a dozen cities across Europe, my precious things are earning interest, have perhaps been earning interest for over a century, in those discreet banks and financial institutions that serve quiet money.

That thought, that I might share a world with my money without knowing, have shared it for all my life, makes my stomach knot. I might be an unknowing millionaire.

Books. A couple—books are heavy; people ask questions of books. I cannot travel without books! I fretted for days before my piles and stacks. Finally I settled on an illustrated Blake and a Herodotus. The best books are the ones I have yet to buy, the ones I will buy out in history. Cheap books made rich by time. I have my eye on a first-edition *Ulysses,* and I know exactly where to find it.

In history. I can't express the excitement and the terror in those words. Not studying history. Not discussing history on some forum or Facebook page, not reading history, not even touching it in diaries, photographs, archives, firsthand experiences, like Thorn's boxes filled with her greygram's cozy war. *In* history. It touching me. Terrifying. The time storm is coming. No dodging, no avoiding, no parleying.

Things in my time traveler's bag I did not pack, which have hitched. Dread. Rootlessness. Adventure. Hope. This is not my home. I feel the heat, taste the car fumes, scent the cooking fats and stray coils of perfumes. I listen to the voices, the traffic rumble, the radio and the rap, the rasp of Vespa engines, the sirens; I take in the sun-bleached stone, the colors of the tiles, the blue of the Virgin's robe in the glass shrine on the corner of Via Aldo Manuzio; the quality of the light and the haze of the sky and the lie of the landscape of clouds, but they aren't mine. I make spaghetti with oil and garlic and chilli and take my coffee in three sips; I discuss football, politics and local scandal at the bar, but I do not belong. I never did; I never will. I would always been that Englishman, foreign, separate, alien. This is not my home. The Fens were not my home. Clapham was an expensive slum, never a home.

Then I try to reach beyond the seductions of the sensual world, to start to a particular electricity, a tingle in the world, a resonance of my body with the reality underlying that of the senses. Entanglement. Tom told me I would know it, and I understand that now. Summer storms flicker over the roof tiles, but they are just electricity. This is not the time; this is not the place. That place will be Shingle Street, and soon, I think. I will stand there and catch one of the harmonics that ripple up and down through time. The doors of history will open and I will be swept through.

Not yet. Not now. Not until I have packed one final item for my bag. A notebook—good, bound in exquisite soft leather, creamy vellum pages that take the ink or pencil with equal facility and grace. Empty now, but I know the title.

I watch the lightning along the edge of the city, lift my pen and write on the first page: *Time Was.*

About the Author

Photograph by Jim C. Hines

IAN MCDONALD was born in 1960 in Manchester, England, to an Irish mother and a Scottish father. He moved with his family to Northern Ireland in 1965. He has won the Locus Award, the British Science Fiction Association Award and the John W. Campbell Memorial Award. He now lives in Belfast.

TOR·COM

Science fiction. Fantasy. The universe.

And related subjects.

*

More than just a publisher's website, *Tor.com* is a venue for **original fiction, comics,** and **discussion** of the entire field of SF and fantasy, in all media and from all sources. Visit our site today—and join the conversation yourself.